Josephine started writing *Divorced and Deadly* as a story on her website, loosely based on true incidents that you couldn't make up if you tried. It proved so popular that the hilarious serial, with exclusive new instalments, is published now as a complete novel.

Josephine is also the author of 39 bestselling novels that have made her a number 1 bestseller and earned her the title of 'the nation's favourite storyteller'.

Her books are available from bookshops and libraries everywhere and you can find out more about them – and catch up with all Jospehine's news – on www.josephinecox.co.uk

Also by Josephine Cox

QUEENIE'S STORY
Her Father's Sins
Let Loose the Tigers

THE EMMA GRADY TRILOGY
Outcast
Alley Urchin
Vagabonds

Angels Cry Sometimes
Take This Woman
Whistledown Woman
Don't Cry Alone
Jessica's Girl
Nobody's Darling
Born to Serve
More than Riches
A Little Badness
Living a Lie
The Devil You Know
A Time for Us
Cradle of Thorns
Miss You Forever
Love Me or Leave Me
Tomorrow the World
The Gilded Cage
Somewhere, Someday
Rainbow Days
Looking Back
Let It Shine

The Woman Who Left
Jinnie

Bad Boy Jack
The Beachcomber
Lovers and Liars
Live the Dream

The Journey
Journey's End
The Loner
Songbird
Born Bad
Divorced and Deadly
Blood Brothers

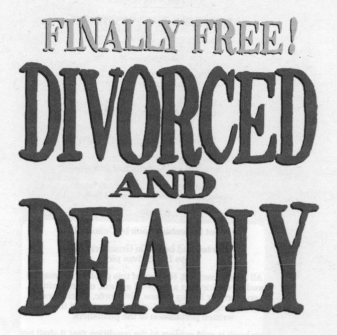

FINALLY FREE!
DIVORCED AND DEADLY

JOSEPHINE COX

HARPER

HARPER

An imprint of HarperCollins*Publishers*
77–85 Fulham Palace Road,
Hammersmith, London W6 8JB

www.harpercollins.co.uk

This paperback edition 2010
1

First published in Great Britain by
HarperCollins*Publishers* 2009

Copyright © Josephine Cox 2009

Josephine Cox asserts the moral right to
be identified as the author of this work

A catalogue record for this book
is available from the British Library

ISBN: 978-0-00-730143-0

rep
in
ph

Th
by
othe
in a
is pi
co

FSC

Mixed Sources
Product group from well-managed
forests and other controlled sources
www.fsc.org Cert no. SW-COC-1806
© 1996 Forest Stewardship Council

FSC is a non-profit international organisation established
to promote the responsible management of the world's forests.
Products carrying the FSC label are independently certified
to assure consumers that they come from forests that are managed
to meet the social, economic and ecological needs
of present and future generations.

Find out more about HarperCollins and the environment at
www.harpercollins.co.uk/green

DEDICATION

With much gratitude to everyone who has ever made me laugh out loud, or told me a funny story that would not go away.

The original idea for this story came when I went to pick my sister up one day. As I turned into her cul-de-sac, I was amazed to see the corner house smothered from top to bottom in huge banners of every colour and description – complete with a massive photograph of a woman in the centre, her fist triumphantly in the air, and a caption saying:

Newly Divorced And Up For Anything!

It got me thinking about all the people I know who've been divorced, where there might be a stalker who can't let go, or one of the party demands everything but the kitchen sink. When new relationships start and jealousy rears its ugly head, the ensuing bitterness can often create unforeseen circumstances, some tragic, some unbelievably funny. My own life, and my set of friends and family were a powerful inspiration for Ben's uproarious account of life after divorce.

I have drawn on the hilarious incidents that happen in real life, to real people, in real situations. At first I put snippets on the website as a temporary relief from life's hardships, a laugh a day to keep the doctor away. But, people loved it! They were signing up in great numbers, and so the publishers in their wisdom decided it must be lengthened into a book, and here it is!

In *Divorced and Deadly*, you'll meet a bunch of characters; some you want to strangle, others you want as your best friend, and some will make you laugh out loud in a crowd, on a train, or just walking along the street.

Divorced and Deadly comes straight out of life; mine included, because anyone who knows me will tell you, I'm a poor diva who causes chaos and destruction wherever I go! I've also got a wicked and vivid imagination, which produced my two crazy, hopeless characters: Ben Buskin, who writes the diary, and his hapless friend, Dickie Manse brains-in-his-pants.

Many thanks to my unsuspecting friends and my wonderful, crazy family; not forgetting all the poor innocents I've sat opposite on a train or a bus. I've been the fly on the wall, recording every hilarious minute.

So enjoy! I've got files of laughter and details of amazing antics that will make you cry with frustration and laugh 'til you ache. So never fear, because there's more to come! And who knows you might even recognise yourself in there!

BEN'S DIARY

BEN'S LOG
WILL SOMEONE PLEASE TELL ME
WHY I'VE BEEN DUMPED?

I'm 36 years old and 'well handsome', with a good head of hair and a pair of kissing lips to die for. I'm not as tall as I'd like to be, but I'd give George Clooney a run for his money. I reckon I'm a better actor than he is, because I played a hippo in *All Creatures Great and Small*. (Anyone with a brain knows how difficult it is to play such a demanding role!)

So, now we all know what a great catch I am – why is it that today my divorce is absolute and I'm out in the cold?

The dreaded Laura doesn't want me any more, and the women who are aching to make a play for me are all too nervous to make the first move, in case Laura rips out their eyes.

To be honest I don't know whether to laugh, cry, or starve the cat for a day… actually no, scrub that last one. (Like all felines she can be vicious, and the last thing I need right now is for her to leap on me from a great height; claws hooked for the kill.)

I'm humiliated. People pity me. You know when you

walk past somebody and they pretend not to have seen you? Or you walk away and the sniggering starts?

Huh! Call themselves friends, I don't think so!

To regain my confidence, I've made a list of things to do:

1. Signing on at the gym is definitely out! (Mainly, because I'm a bit short of the old readies. Also, Dickie told me that too much exercise can ruin your love life.) Mind you, what does Dickie Manse brains in his pants know about anything?

2. I'll smoke cigars instead of cigarettes, because they're sexier. My Dad's got an old film of Jimmy Cagney, where he's smoking a cigar. There's a trail of smoke curling up from his lips, and one eye half shut like he's winking, (truth is, I reckon he can't see a damned thing through that smoke!) Even so, does he look the cool dude or what?

3. When the opposite sex look at me in that certain way... (you always know when they're eyeing you up!) I'll cunningly avert my gaze and play hard to get; (anyway, I'm a bit short-sighted, so I need to look where I'm going.)

4. I intend taking two vitamins a day; one evening prim-
   rose, because it's said to smooth out your wrinkles
   and brighten your eyes. Oh, and I'll take a large ghinko
   biloba tablet (Dickie Manse brains in his pants said he
   sprouted hairs on his chest after only one course!) I'm
   not worried about a hairy chest, but if I'm lucky, who
   knows what *else* might 'pop up'?)

5. I will not contact Laura in any way, shape or form. (That
   does not count most evenings when I hide in the
   bushes, to see who she's messing about with! It's my
   right! After all, it wasn't me who did the dumping!)

6. Oh, and to keep up my self-esteem, I will admire myself in
   the mirror every morning. I'll do a bit of flexing
   and puffing, and whatever else is necessary,in order
   to keep the image up. (Yes, that an' all)

Right! That's enough of the good intentions. I need to
keep sharp, and concentrate my mind for the trauma
ahead.

I know for certain that Laura is laughing behind
my back. I sneaked past the house earlier on today and

judging by the massive placards and banners plastered all over the front of the house, on the gate and down the street – she's having a ball, proclaiming to all and sundry in large, colourful letters that she is:

Newly Divorced And Up For Anything

'Up for anything'. What's that supposed to mean, as if I didn't know. This is her way of taking a snide jab at me, the spiteful cow! She's never forgotten that one miserable time when I lost it … if you know what I mean? I tried to explain it to her, but she was having none of it … you know how women can whine when they want to… 'You just don't love me any more, that's the truth isn't it?'

And, no, that is *not* the truth! The truth is, I'd been out with the boys and drunk myself under the table … well it *was* Trevor's stag-night after all, and besides, I reckon Wayne spiked my drinks because his wife fancies me. (If truth be told, it's the same old story of jealousy and spite!)

All the same, if I thought Laura still had lingering feelings for me, I might lie through my teeth and tell her I deserve everything she throws at me, and that I'll never go anywhere without her again. The thing is, I still love her you see … or I think I do. Or maybe I don't. God, she's right! I'm just a hopeless mess.

I'm no angel. She knew that when she married me. I've never claimed to be anything other than an absolute rogue, and I won't apologise for that. In my book, women have a role to play in the home and bed, while every man on God's earth has a God-given right to play the field if he wants to. I mean, where's the harm, tell me that?

Would you believe, she even went so far as to suggest I might be unhinged. Well, I've got news for her. It's not *me* who's unhinged, it's her!

Talk about over reacting. I mean, when she found me in our bed with another woman she threw me out! I suppose it was inevitable. Mind you, Laura didn't even give me time to explain. Y'see, I didn't know who the woman was. I couldn't even recall whether I picked her up at the pub, or rescued her from the bus stop when her bus was late. Anyway, suffice to say we ended up in bed, and Laura found us. Worse luck!

There was no way she would listen to reason. She just threw all my clothes out on the street and me with them. I don't know what happened to the girl, but it wouldn't surprise me if she wasn't dead and buried under our garage floor.

Honestly! Laura just went crazy. Totally and absolutely out of control, like frothing mad. It was really off-putting.

And it was the coldest night imaginable, and there *I* was, stark-naked except for my odd-coloured socks (that's another thing! How she manages to put four pairs of socks into the washing machine and lose one sock from each pair, I will never know).

I kid you not! That night, I saw a side to her that I'd never seen before, and never want to see again. It was not a pleasant sight.

I mean, what's got into her? She didn't flare up like that the time she caught me snogging her best friend, Shelley. Instead she gave Shelley a black eye before booting her out on her ear, yet she made me suffer for months before my penalty was served! (It goes without saying, Shelley is not her best friend any more.)

In fact, Shelley is *nobody's* best mate, especially now, when all the women in the street have it in for her. Mind you I'm not surprised, because they all fancied a tumble with me, and Shelley beat them to it. Lucky me, eh?

Our marriage should have ended there and then, but Laura forgave me in the end. So what made her end it, just after half an hours' harmless frolicking with a stranger I'd only just met?

I can't believe how Laura reacted. I mean! There was no need to go berserk. I kept telling her, it was all just a bit of fun, that's all it was.

Well, I mean to say, I can't help it if I'm irresistible to women, can I? We all know some men have it and some don't. I just happen to have it.

I am no longer married. Sadly, I've had to move in with my parents, and yes, they did give me a hard time. 'You've only yourself to blame,' that was Dad. 'When will you ever learn?' that was Mum.

And as if that wasn't enough, they'd been gossiping with the dog about their disapproval of my nocturnal goings on. So he took it upon himself to sink his canines into my leg and draw blood. (I'll get him for that when they're not looking!)

Mind you, I can't really blame him, the poor sod had 'em chopped off last week, so now his days of impressing the pretty thing with his massive ego and other jangly bits are well and truly over.

Hell's bells, I've just had a frightening thought ... were they planning to do the same to me? Like creep up on me while I was asleep, and nip my pride in the bud! (Dad won the neatest bush competition last year, so he really knows his way around the garden shears.)

You probably think I'm paranoid, and you'd be right. I wouldn't put it past them to rob me of my manhood. The thing is, they're in their sixties now and have probably forgotten what joy it all is.

Anyway, I don't plan to stay there long; although I have to admit, it's a good gaff: no rent, hot meals provided, bed changed regularly, with clean shirts and underpants on hand.

I can't help but wonder if Dad's feeling put out, 'You'll be wiping his backside next!' he snapped at Mum the other day, 'And why is it he always bags the bathroom first?'

Huh! *I* can answer that ... it's because Dad has a nasty habit of leaving his false teeth on the sink after he's washed them; it's unnerving, seeing his false teeth grinning at me when I'm on the throne.

'C'mon our Ben.' That's Mum again. 'You'd best get off or you'll be late.' I argued a bit and wolfed down my hot crumpets oozing with butter and jam, while she hovered over me with a bag of goodies. 'I've packed you some nice ham sandwiches,' she cooed. 'Oh, and there's a bottle of Lucozade in there, it'll keep your pecker up.' (Does she know something I don't?)

Well anyway, there I was, on my way up the street, swinging my goodies like a kid off to school. I wondered why she didn't put me in short pants and get me a cap with a badge!

Then, as if things weren't bad enough, I saw that twerp from number fourteen – Dickie Manse brains-in-his-pants. I have to say, I've never seen such an unholy mess – long and limp with a sprout of hair on top and short trousers at the bottom; he'd be a real attraction at Madame Tussauds.

He ran as fast as he could to catch me up. 'God! You walk fast, don't you?' he said, breathlessly running alongside, 'I thought I'd never catch up!'

All the way to the bus stop he asked questions, 'Where's your car?'

'It went in for a service and they've discovered it needs new brake pads. Hopefully, I should have it back tomorrow.'

'Ah, well, if you ask me, it's all a con.'

'Is that so?' If he doesn't clear off soon, I swear I'd smack him one! Either that or I'd tell my mum and she'd give him what for.

'Think about it.' Like a dog with a bone, he is. 'You've never noticed anything wrong with your brakes at all, have you?'

'Not that I can remember, no.'

What the hell was I talking to him for? It only encouraged him.

'There you are then!'

'*Where* am I exactly?'

'Well, like I say … you've been conned. There's nothing wrong with your brakes at all.'

'Isn't there?'

'No. You see, what they'll do is whip 'em off. One of the blokes will have 'em away, and before you know it, there they are…'

'*Where* are they?' Talk about being a glutton for punishment.

'On the stall at a car-boot sale o' course!'

'Really?' No wonder he's called Dickie Manse brains-in-his-pants.

His tongue was still rattling ten to the dozen when the bus arrived. Pushing me aside, he climbed on, while I pretended to tie my shoe. When the bus pulled away Dickie started waving and yelling and telling them to stop because they'd left me behind. (Thick as a plank or what!)

The conductor was in no mood for his antics. I expect he was wondering why I was smiling after being left behind. Good man, that conductor! The thing is, I'd rather be late than sit next to Dickie Manse brains-in-his-pants all the way to work.

After I'd thrown what was left of my little-boy's lunch, I started to wonder ... what was going to happen to me now? How will I get over Laura, especially as Shelley won't have anything to do with me after all the goings on.

And how long will I have to stay at my parents' house?

A long time I reckon, because Laura fleeced me good and proper, my Ford Focus is about to give up the ghost, and all I've got is a fiver in my back pocket and exactly four pounds and sixty pence in my bank account.

Still, I've got my magnetic looks, and I still know how to make a lady feel good.

Then I noticed a woman looking at me. She was tall and blonde with legs all the way up to her chin.

Now she's started walking towards me! Keep calm, Ben. Play it cool ... cool now. I said, 'Hello... yes, did you want something?' Realising I sounded like Dickie Manse, I gave her my best, whitest smile.

'Look...' she pointed downwards.

I looked down and saw nothing untoward, except a slight stirring.

'Hope you don't mind me saying ... I just thought I'd tell you that your shoelaces were undone.' She walked straight into the open arms of a man who was running up to meet her. She gave me this bemused little smile as he walked her away.

I could hear the pair of them sniggering all the way down the street. Not that I cared a toss. I didn't fancy her anyway.

I've decided to look on the positive side.

What's the worst that can happen? I mean, I can handle Dickie Manse brains-in-his-pants, a sniggering blonde, a bad divorce, stolen brake pads, clean underpants and a bottle of Lucozade to 'keep my pecker up'.

It'll take more than that to bring Ben Buskin to his knees.

I was determined to come out on top. Yes! Just you see if I don't.

BEDFORD
OCTOBER, THURSDAY

Hello diary, my old friend.

Well, like I've always said, you never know what's round the corner. I had a couple of surprises today; both involving women of course. One was a bit unnerving, and the other positively amazing. I still don't quite know what to make of it all.

I reckon I must have done something very wrong in a previous life, or I wouldn't be punished the way I'm being punished now.

I arrived at the station at nine a.m., right on time. Most times the damned train is late, and other times I find myself stranded on some scary platform in the middle of nowhere! Anyway, not this time; although the train driver must have had an argument with his wife, because he was whizzing over the rails like a demented hooligan.

'I think I'm about to be sick, dear!' The fat woman sitting

next to me had already fallen asleep on my shoulder, but it wasn't her fault, as she had a droopy neck; or so she told me when I shook her awake.

'You'd best sit up,' I told her encouragingly, '…I'll see if I can find the conductor.' The last thing I wanted was to turn up for work with a jacket coated in the remains of her breakfast!

'Give her a sick bag!' The conductor was none too pleased, and neither was I.

'Give her one yourself!' I mean … you can't let the buggers get away with it, can you?

Anyway, to cut a long story short, she got her sick bag, and I got as far away from her as I could; though she kept looking at me with a peculiar glint in her eye. 'Sorry dear,' I wanted to say, 'but I'm not that desperate.' At least, not yet! How dare she?

What's more, a muscled-up weirdo with a crew-cut on the next seat kept eyeing me up. I nearly asked her what *her* game was!

Thank God I got to my station unmolested … life is a terrifying lottery, don't you think?

The van was waiting to collect me as I came out of the station. 'Good morning, Ben, how was your journey today?' Dressed in a long, white overall and smelling of dog-chuckles, Poppy is a real sweetie; though you wouldn't want to kiss her after she's been canoodling with the canines.

Feeling sorry for myself, I climbed in. 'It's been one of

them journeys from hell,' I moaned. 'The train driver was hell bent on breaking every speed limit in the book, and some woman was threatening to spew up all over me.' I gave her all the gory details, 'And would you believe the conductor had a go at me when I refused to take her the sick bag!'

'Really? And what did you say to that?' she asked. Poppy can be such a trial at times.

'What do you *think* I said? I calmly reminded him that I was a mere passenger, and that it was *his* duty to "give her one"!'

Poppy started laughing. Honestly! Is it me, or has the whole world gone completely mad?

As we drove along, I took a sneaky look at her. Some people say Poppy is quite pretty, but I can't quite make up my mind. I suppose with her wild, curly hair and those long, blonde lashes over sapphire-blue eyes, there might be something cute about her.

But then, who am I to say? She's so preoccupied with her dungarees and other people's animals; I can't imagine her being dressed to kill, or rolling about in bed playing catch me if you can with another human being. And she would never flaunt herself naked in a see-through negligee … or would she? I'd better watch out. There I go again with the daydreams!

'What are you staring at?' Poppy asked.

'What d'you mean? I wasn't staring at you!' I can sound really wounded when I put my mind to it.

'Well it certainly *felt* like it!' She flew the car round the bend at a hundred miles an hour.

Leave her alone, Ben, I told myself, before she kills the pair of us.

'I've already said … I was *not* staring at you!' I reacted with a cutting remark.

'No need to be catty.' She seemed hurt.

'What do you mean … catty?' I said. 'I'm a man for heavens' sake. I couldn't be catty if I tried. The trouble is that's all you've got on your mind … cats and dogs, and things that cock their leg over … other things.'

'What other things?' Poppy wanted to know.

'I dunno … plant pots, trees, and things like that.'

'Now you're being ridiculous.' Poppy obviously didn't think so!

'Leave me alone, I've had a bad enough morning already!' I was not in a pleasant frame of mind.

'Oh what! You mean you forgot to feed your Mum's goldfish?'

She was giving me that kind of grin she gives the animals when they want feeding, I half expected a meaty-chew thrust into my mouth, thank you very much!

'You know what's wrong with *you*, Ben?' Poppy went on.

'No, but I'm sure you'll tell me.' Why did I say that?

'You need to chill out.' Poppy said.

'What's that supposed to mean?' I put on my most out-raged voice.

Putting the fear of God into me, she screeched the van to a halt in the middle of the street, 'You listen to me…' Yanking on the hand-brake she swung round and looked me in the eye, 'You're on edge all the time; it's not good for you. People have heart attacks and everything, being on edge like that.'

'I can't help it. I've got a lot to contend with.' My mum was right. I really *can* be sulky at times.

'You might be surprised to know this, but you are not the only one!' Poppy complained.

'What?' I didn't know what she was on about.

'I said, you are not the only one who has a lot to contend with.' She was really ranting!

'Is that so?' Now I was fed up.

'What about me?' Poppy went on.

'I don't know. What about you?' I really hadn't a clue.

'You know…' Poppy said mournfully, '…my favourite dog passed away last week, and you never once said you were sorry.'

'That's because I wasn't.' It's true! 'That dog was not even yours. What's more, he was mad as a march hare … eight times last week it escaped and I was the one who had to catch it and bring it back … plus I got bitten twice for my trouble and had to have a jab.' I couldn't believe we were arguing about a mad dog!

'Don't be soft! A jab won't hurt you, will it? And besides, you were the only one available to go after the poor thing.

Everyone else was busy hosing out the kennels after that bug epidemic.' Poppy could be really verbal!

'All right, but losing one dog in the universe does not give you as much to contend with as I have.' I had to assert myself.

'Oh no? Well, what about my mother?' Poppy gave me a look.

'What about her ... and don't you think we'd best get going or we'll be late. Don't forget the accountant is due in today.' And guess who had to deal with him – yours truly!

'I haven't forgotten.' Poppy sounded smug.

'Let's get going then.' The morning was definitely not getting any better!

She didn't get going until the driver in the car behind rammed his fist on his horn, and then a milk float and a bread van drew up behind us and soon there was a whole mob of vehicles all lined up and baying for blood.

And even after we drove away, she had no intention of letting me off the hook.

'I'll have you know, my mother is the mother from hell!' Poppy complained.

'Really? In what way?' I didn't particularly want to pursue the conversation, but I couldn't believe her mother was worse than mine.

'She vets all my boyfriends.' Poppy said.

'I didn't know you had any *boyfriends*.' I almost laughed.

I got the evil eye, 'And why shouldn't I have boyfriends. Am I ugly? Tell me the truth; do you think I'm ugly? You do, don't you ... think I'm ugly?' Her voice was suspiciously shaky.

'I never said that.' Honest!

'But you meant that,' she sniffed.

'I didn't.' What else could I say?

'Liar!' Poppy was almost in tears.

When we arrived at the kennel gates I couldn't get out of the van quick enough to open them. 'It's all right,' I called as she prepared to stop and collect me again, 'I'll walk up ... clear my head.'

'Please yourself!' With the same death wish as the train driver, she slammed her foot down on the accelerator and shot off up the lane, sending showers of gravel behind her.

'DAMNED LUNATIC! YOU COULD HAVE BLINDED ME!' I yelled.

She didn't hear me. Well, I knew that, or I wouldn't have shouted, would I? I mean ... *I'm* not harbouring a death wish, well, at least not yet.

Oh yes, and what were the 'surprises' you might ask.

Well, as you might have guessed, I manage a kennel for some rich guy who has a string of them all over the UK. He has a big white house on a cliff-top in Spain, a grand mansion in Milton Keynes and a boat in Newquay. Huh! alright for some!

I'm learning the ropes so I can achieve fame and fortune; though so far it's been an uphill struggle.

While I was preparing the books for the accountant, I had a visitor. Imagine my astonishment when I looked up and saw her draped in the doorway, half-naked boobs peeping out like fat puppies from a sack, and her cheap, heady perfume blocking my common sense. 'SHELLEY! What are you doing here?' In the midst of chaos, I always managed to find a semblance of authority.

'I came to see you,' she purred, stepping closer.

Backing away, I told her in no uncertain terms, 'Haven't you women done enough damage? I've lost my home and my marriage, and now I'm back with my parents who think I still need my nose wiping. Thanks to you lot, my life's a mess and there's no way out.'

She didn't answer. Neither did she show any remorse, the spiteful cow. Instead, she sauntered right up to me; thrusting her large, fleshy boobs into my chest and wrapping her snake-like arms round my neck. She kissed me full on the lips … right there, tongue out, tonsils quivering, with four kennel-girls and the dog-walkers staring in at the window.

'GET OFF ME!' Blushing to the roots of my hair, I shoved her away, masterfully taking hold of her arm to march her out the door.

'You can throw me out of your office, but you will never be able to push me out of your life,' she warned. 'You're a

28

free man now. You and I belong together, and I won't let you go, Ben. It's no use you fighting me.' With that she blew me a kiss and wiggled away down the lane and out of sight.

'Clear off! Haven't you lot got work to do?' The kennel-girls and dog-walkers were still there, peering in the window and giggling crudely.

'Cor, just think, Ben...' That was Poppy with her nose pressed so hard to the window it was covered in a film of snot, '...that Shelley is head over heels in love with you. I reckon you could have asked her to turn somersaults and she would have done, right there on the spot.'

'Huh!' That was the new boy, Andy. 'If you ask me, she's anybody's!' He gave one of the idiot grins he's getting known for. 'I don't think it's you, Ben. I think she just wanted to play, and d'you know what? If I'd been brave enough to give her the nod, I bet you, she'd have been all over me...'

Well, that was it! I just lost my rag, 'What d'you think this is ... a bloody peep-show ... GET BACK TO YOUR WORK, THE LOT OF YOU!'

Well, I never ... they all shot off in different directions. So! I do have a masterful streak when I make my mind up.

So, maybe from now on they'll learn to respect me.

Not so! Because that same afternoon, I was preparing to leave, when I had another visitor, unannounced and baying for blood, 'YOU FILTHY TWO-TIMING NO GOOD BAGGAGE!'

My ex-wife was never more attractive than when fighting mad, 'Don't think you and that slut have got one over on me, because you haven't. She's been bragging all over the place, about how she means to have you. Well, I'm telling you now, she's welcome to you … and good luck to the pair of you!'

With that she stormed off with me running after her, 'What the hell business is it of yours anyway?' I didn't care that the kennel-girls were staring at us, 'You were the one who asked for a divorce and never mind that I didn't want it. So don't come here with your high-faluting values, telling me what I can and can't do. I shall do what I damn well like, and with whoever I please! And if you don't like it, then tough tittie!'

I swear I didn't see it coming. She swung round, grabbed the hose from young Danny's hand and turned it on me. There was a great whoosh, a blinding curtain of freezing cold rain, and my whole body was soaked to the skin. She then flung the hose back to Danny who ran about like a lunatic, trying to catch it, as it leaped up and down swilling everybody in sight.

The girls were laughing and screaming, and poor Danny came off worse when with a look of triumph he deliberately trod on the hose, which then forced itself up his trouser leg and gave him the biggest surprise of his life.

Humiliated and dripping, and wishing I was a million miles away, I watched Laura storm off with a sinister warning, 'I know she was here, Ben Buskin. And I'll be watching you!'

Like one of the half-dead creatures from Michael Jackson's *Thriller*, I hobbled after her, 'How did you know she was here … are you spying on me?'

'Yes! Same as you're spying on me. Do you think I haven't seen you hiding in the shrubs to see what I'm up to … DAMN PERVERT!' She screamed.

With the weight of my wet trousers pulling me down I sulked back to the office, where I slammed about like a sulky kid who's lost the fight.

'Here … let me help.' Poppy had seen it all, and as always she was there to pick up the pieces. Before I could stop her, she'd stripped off my trousers (taking far too long if you ask me). Then she wrapped a fluffy dog-blanket round my nether regions and was about to rub my chest with a flannel, when I thanked her kindly and sent her away … I mean, I've already got more trouble than I can handle.

But all in all, it was a day to remember.

What puzzles me is this … why would my ex-wife get herself in such a state when she's already divorced me?

Maybe she still loves me.

Well, well. Whoever would have thought it?

Mind you, tomorrow could tell *another* tale.

BEDFORD
OCTOBER, FRIDAY

'Ben!' Mum's voice screamed up the stairs, 'Ben, it's time for work.'

'Go away.' Covering my head with the sheet I did my best to ignore her.

'Ben!' Ignore her.

'Ben, are you awake?' Double ignore her.

'BEN … it's half past eight, you'll miss your bus!' Dammit!

'ALL RIGHT, ALL RIGHT! I'M ONTO IT!' I yelled.

There was a long pause. I knew instinctively she was at the bottom of the stairs, coiled and hissing, ready for the kill.

With a groan I leaned out of bed, fished my shoe out from under the chair and banged it three times on the floor. That usually got me another ten minutes.

God, am I tired. Thank heavens it's Friday. It's my

Saturday off this week, and I'm brimming with ideas. I plan to trawl the clubs and pubs and find a woman who will take care of me.

I am *not* going to go to the cinema with Dickie Manse brains-in-his-pants. He must think I'm stupid. Why would anyone in their right mind want to go to the cinema with a saddo like that?

My weekend plans were interrupted by hideous yelling. 'BEN! IF YOU ARE NOT OUT OF THAT BED AND DOWN HERE IN FIVE MINUTES FLAT, I SWEAR I'LL COME UP AND DRAG YOU OUT!'

She won't. She's said that before. What's more, my clock said quarter to eight … she'd played that trick on me before. Let her shout and rave, I knew I was good for at least another five minutes yet.

I heard on the grapevine that Shelley has been putting it about to anyone who'll listen, that me and her are an item. Brazen-faced liar! I can see I'll have to pay her a call and put her in her place once and for all. If she thinks she can play me along and sort my life out without my permission, she's got another thing coming!

'I KNEW IT!' The door was flung open and there she was … my mother in full war paint. 'Your father's gone to get a haircut, and I'm off shopping with Winnie Arriss … if you don't mind I would like to get to the shops before they close.' With a swoop she was on me… Grabbing the bedclothes, she flung them back with no thought whatsoever for my bared manhood, not to mention my red face.

'OUT!' God she was a frightening sight; standing there arms folded, face like a bulldog and frothing at the mouth.

Covering my modesty, I gave her one of my fiercest stares, 'I don't know what all the fuss is about.'

Casting her gaze down, she snorted, 'Neither do I.'

'Look! It's not even eight o'clock!' I pointed at my bed-side clock, 'See?'

Grabbing the clock she gave it a shake and threw it at me, just missing my head. 'You forgot to wind it up again. How many times have I told you, being as it was your Grandma's … Lord rest her soul … it needs winding up every day…' As she went out the room, she added snidely, 'That clock and you belong together. Grown lazy with age, the pair of you.'

It took me ten minutes to finish in the bathroom, though when I came out I looked like a refugee from a war zone. I had patches of blood and sticky paper all over my face and my hair stood up like it had been through a wind tunnel. 'It's your fault,' I sulked as I came into the kitchen where my mother was waiting with another packed lunch.

'You've got no time for breakfast now,' she said lovingly. (One minute she's going crazy, and the next she's sweet as apple pie. I'm sure she's an alien.)

'Anyway, I've put you an extra apple in, and one of them choccy biscuits you seem to like so much.' (She doesn't know those revolting choccy biscuits are the first thing to go in the bin when I got to the bus stop.)

I grabbed my coat and made for the door. I didn't want to give her the idea that she can shout at me, and then just forget it, like it never happened.

'Look, Ben, I'm sorry for shouting at you, but you really have got to pull yourself together.' (She can read my mind!) You've lost your wife; you don't seem to be making much headway at work ... I mean, look at the state you came home in the other day.'

'What state was that?' I was in no mood to give in.

'Your suit appeared to have shrunk and your best leather shoes were all wrinkly; not an image you want to present to the customers. And what's more, you have no home, no ambition, and very few prospects for the future.' She made that sad face, 'What's going to become of you, Ben?'

By the time I got out the door, my self-confidence was shattered, my self-image had taken a real knocking, and my heart was in my boots.

Walking down the street muttering to myself, I realised she was right. I was kidding myself. I was a joke at work, nobody respected what I had to say, and if the boss sold up tomorrow, I'd be out of a job. I was already broke. I had one woman spreading lies and chasing me at every turn, and another who said she doesn't want me, but has threatened

36

to kill me if another woman even looked in my direction. Then there's Poppy, who'll nag me to death, even though she fancies me rotten. But she's just a kid, and besides I've heard her shamelessly rattling them off in the yard … how off-putting is that?' Some lady she is, I must say!

I wasn't bothered if I missed the bus, or even got to work at all; I leaned against the wall, wondering if anyone would care if I ended things right here and now.

'Hey!' It was Dickie Manse brains-in-his-pants.

'What d'you think you're doing lolling against the wall like you've all the time in the world? The bus is coming in … look!' Grabbing my arm he ran me all the way down to the bus stop. I must have dropped my precious lunch box because when we scrambled on to the bus, there was no sign of it. Oh, God! No little-boy lunch box! The day was already brightening. Perhaps I won't end it after all; well, not just yet anyway.

'Hey!' Giving me a dig in the ribs, Dickie Manse brains-in-his-pants was going on about some girl he met at the cinema. 'Sat next to me she did,' any little thing pleased him. 'I offered her some of my popcorn and she dug in like a little trooper.'

I pretended to listen, but to tell the truth, I was a bit jealous. How does he do it? He's long and thin, wiry as a whippet with a pineapple-top hairdo, yet there he was, sitting quietly in his seat at the cinema, when the girl next to him dipped into his goodies. No strings or conditions, just casual like.

'Really?' I wasn't all that interested. 'And did it go any-where?'

'What?' Staring at me with fish eyes he looked evil.

'I said … did it go anywhere? I mean, did you kiss her? Did you take her home afterwards?'

'No.' He looked embarrassed.

'No … what?' I wasn't going to let this go!

'No, I didn't kiss her.' He was looking shifty now.

'Why not?' I persisted.

Just then the conductor came for the fare. (It's high time this lame government did something about public transport. In any civilised country, public transport to work should be free.)

Under protest, we paid the fare and when the conduc-tor moved on, I prodded Dickie Manse brains-in-his-pants, 'Well?'

'Well … what?' I could see he was trying to avoid the subject.

'Why didn't you kiss her?' I said.

'Because I … didn't, that's all.' He wouldn't look at me.

There was something strange going on here, I thought. 'Ah, I see!'

'No! It's not what you think … she didn't slap my face or anything like that. In fact we got on really well … until…' He blushed deep scarlet.

'Until what?' I had noticed on other occasions that when he gulped, his Adam's apple bobbed frantically up and down. Right now, it was going up and down so fast, it was like one of them balls in the Lotto draw.

'Look, Ben, I know I like the girls, and sometimes they like me, and that's fine. But sometimes it just doesn't work out. So if I tell you the truth, you won't laugh, will you … because if you laugh, I'll feel worse than I feel now and frankly I feel terrible.'

'Crikey, Dickie … you didn't try it on did you … right there in the cinema? I mean, she didn't raise the alarm did she, and get you thrown out?' Already I was beginning to chuckle. Sometimes he can be a right prat.

'No, that's not what happened, and I'm not saying any more, because I knew you'd laugh. You always do!'

There was a moment of silence between us. He didn't stop biting his lip, while I was thinking how it served him right, because he thinks he's God's gift and at the end of the day he's just a pathetic loser, like me.

'Ben?' Dickie said in a small voice.

'Now what?' Honestly!

'You think I'm a loser, don't you?' he continued.

'Course not, why ever would I think that?' That's twice today somebody's read my mind. Ooh!

Dickie seemed to think about it. 'So, you won't laugh if I tell you what happened, will you?'

'I've already said, haven't I?' It was like talking to a brick wall!

This time the heavy silence lasted until just as we were almost at our destiantion.

He wasn't comfortable with the idea of telling me, so I didn't push it. Besides, I had other things on my mind: would Shelley turn up at the kennels? What if Laura showed her face? And as for Poppy ... well, what should I do about Poppy? She has this silly crush on me. But like I said ... I'm naturally popular; though if it goes on for long enough, it's likely to get tiresome.

Once we were on solid ground and rushing along, Dickie Manse brains-in-his-pants slipped in the news, 'I did try and go a bit further after we shared my popcorn.'

'Yes, I gathered that. And she slapped your face, caused a riot and you got thrown out. You took it too far before she was ready ... like you always do. Now, that's the truth isn't it?'

'No, she was ready for anything.' Dickie said. 'She kissed me full on the mouth, I got excited, slid my hand up her skirt, and for a minute I thought she was wearing woolly knickers, but they weren't knickers. It was frightening! Her name wasn't Pam, it was Sam, and it was *me* who caused the riot thanks to her ... *him*, it was *me* who got thrown out.'

I managed to keep calm until he hurried off, and I was on my way up the drive to the kennels. Then my mind was alive with the image of Dickie with his hands up another man's skirt. And God forgive me, I couldn't help it. I was still laughing as I came into the yard; though laughter turned into a yell of horror when I skidded on some dog mess and ended up in the horse trough.

'Oh, my! Are you all right?' Poppy must have had her binoculars out. 'Oh, Ben, you poor thing … let me help you.'

Here we go again!

Another day, another simple lesson to be learned.

Do not laugh at Dickie Manse brains-in-his-pants, because you could end up in the horse trough or worse!

BEDFORD
OCTOBER, MONDAY

I feel uneasy.

Laura did not show up at the kennels today. There has been no sign of rampant Shelley, and as always, Poppy is still on the prowl. (I don't know why she doesn't just buy herself a dog and walk off all that raw energy.)

As for Dickie Manse brains-in-his-pants, he's a walking disaster! Remember how he accidentally on purpose put his groping hand up that girl's skirt, and then discovered it wasn't a girl at all? Well, according to him, he has now found himself a 'proper girl', and he's absolutely besotted. 'You've got to meet her,' he came running down the street at me. 'Her name is Leonora, and she's so good looking, it's unbelievable. And she really likes me!' (I told him not to get too excited, because I know how easily excitement can turn to horror. But would he listen? Of course not.)

'Good. I'm pleased for you.' As always I did my best to humour him. 'But don't go rushing it or you'll frighten her off.'

He drooled and gabbled all the way down the street. 'She's got a friend,' he said. 'Her name's Georgie and she's looking for someone. We could all go out on a date. So? What d'you think?'

I told him what I thought, in no uncertain terms. 'You know what a frightening time I've been through … and am *still* going through,' I reminded him, 'so, what makes you think I need to mess my life up even more. I hope you're not up to your old tricks again.'

'What d'you mean?' Dickie looked put out.

'I mean … "she" is not a "he" … is she?' I queried.

Blushing bright crimson, he took the hump. 'I knew you'd never let me live that down!' he declared sulkily. 'I'll have to remember not to confide in you any more. Anyway you're barking up the wrong tree as usual. Her name is really Georgina. They just call her Georgie for short.'

We walked on in silence.

Poppy was waiting for me as I got off the train. 'Oh, Ben, I'm so excited. I've had a birth; six boys and a girl!'

'Well done,' I told her. 'As you haven't even got a boyfriend, that's an amazing achievement.'

She giggled in a way that made me want to cuddle her. 'No, silly! It's Dizzy, the dog … she belongs to that old man who's gone away for three weeks. He's due back next Friday.'

44

'Timed it well, didn't he?' It's happened before. Some irresponsible owner lets the dog out; the local big boy cocks his leg over and before you know it, things are a stirring. The owner doesn't want the mess and worry, so he dumps the pregnant bitch at the kennels and conveniently forgets to tell us there's a happy event due any minute. Poppy protested, 'we could see she was about to drop the puppies, but we couldn't turn them away could we?'

'Come on then.' Spurring myself into a run, I went into the kennel and there, all curled up round their haggard mummy, was a clutch of the most darling little runts you can imagine. 'I'm sorry, Poppy, but they'll have to go!' At times like this, I had to be hard.

Poppy started wailing and crying. (A girl in floods of tears always turns me to jelly.)

'All right, STOP THAT!' That's the way to treat them.

'So, can we keep them then?' She pleaded.

'Absolutely not!' I held firm.

'Please?'

'Oh, all right then. But only until the owner gets back. This is not a nursery. The old fox must have known she was about to drop a bundle, and he never said a word.'

'He may not have known.' Poppy can be so gullible at times.

'Whether he knew or not, they're here and we need him to collect them. Oh, and you can add another ten per cent onto the bill.'

'But they're not costing us anything!' Poppy wailed.

'Who's the boss here?' I demanded.

There was a sniff. 'You are.'

'Too right. And I will not have these kennels being used as a nursery for randy animals. My answer is final, and that's that.'

'Don't do it, Ben! He's just an old pensioner, and that's so cruel.' I could see the tears welling again.

'Oh, all right then … make it five per cent.' What am I like?

Something has got to change. It seems like I'm always painting myself into a corner.

I have this theory that in order to assert my authority at work, I need to have a stable and worry free home life. And to do that, I need to start looking for a rented place. But because I can't afford to do that on my own, I might need to find a flatmate.

For one heart-stopping minute there, I thought of Dickie Manse brains-in-his-pants.

What a nightmare *that* would be!

BEDFORD
OCTOBER, SATURDAY

I think my mother has finally flipped.

All day she couldn't do enough for me. 'Would you like another cup of tea, Ben darling?'

'No, thanks all the same, Mother.'

'Well, I made us a Madeira cake last night, how about a slice of that?'

'I'm not hungry, Mother. That stew you made filled me up to the eyes. But thanks all the same.'

'Right, well, I'm off to the shops now. I've seen a lovely blue shirt in Jackson's window. I'll buy it for you, shall I?'

'I don't need a shirt, Mother.'

'Why not?'

'Because I bought two new ones last week, don't you remember? It was you who told me where to find the best bargains.'

'Did I?' She's got this irritating habit of frantically

scratching her head until her hair stands on end. She did it then, 'I think you must be mistaken, dear.'

'No, I'm not. Why don't you ask Dad? He'll tell you.'

'Dad?' Isn't it strange how parents call each other Mum and Dad when they've got children? It's like the kids have stolen their identity.

That settles it! I am never going to have kids!

My name is Ben. Not husband, or father or Dad. It's Ben, and that's that!

Dad looked up from his beloved newspaper. 'Yes, Mother, what is it?' (Why does he call her his mother … she's not his mother, she's his wife. Has he forgotten her name, or what?)

'Did I send our Ben to Jackson's shop last week to buy two shirts?' She demanded.

'You did, yes.' Dad sounded resigned.

'Are you sure?' Mum wasn't about to let it go.

'Positive.' Came the reply.

'I see!' She gave me one of her looks. 'All right! Well, if your father says it's so, then I suppose it must be right. But I'll buy you another shirt anyway. You can never have enough shirts.' She punched father's newspaper. 'Isn't that right?'

'For pity's sake!' Dad complained. 'Can't a man read a paper in peace?'

'I said … a man can never have enough shirts.' What is wrong with the woman?

'If you say so, dear.' Dad knew when to give in.

'I do.' Mother smiled triumphantly.

Dad settled himself in his chair. 'Then that's settled. Now, can I please read my paper?'

'If you must!'

At times like this, sharing a flat with Dickie Manse brains-in-his-pants looks very tempting.

BEDFORD
OCTOBER, SUNDAY

I thought I deserved a lie in as I'd had a hard week at work. On Thursday, two cats almost tore each other to shreds when Poppy accidentally shut them in together. That same afternoon, young Simon took the Great Dane for a walk and it ran off with him. Simon ended up in the duck pond; the dog leaped into the baker's back garden, flattened a hutch and sent the four rabbits into the undergrowth. He chased them down a hole, and it took three men two hours to retrieve them.

And there's more! By late afternoon, I'd actually finished extending the puppy run. When Agnes Dovecote arrived with her snappy Dachsund, she somehow managed to fall into the hole, which I'd dug in the wrong place and forgotten to cover. I always believed she was some kind of lady, but I must tell you, I have never heard such shocking language in all my life. After twisting her ankle and laddering her tights (more like flight-path balloons), the old biddy cunningly blackmailed me into letting her 'darling toots' have a fortnight's stay at my expense (I didn't know who to throttle first ... the snappy Dachsund or the old cow!).

And now, what with all that digging, there's not one inch of my poor body that doesn't ache.

My Granny's old alarm clock has taken on a life of its own. Mum should have binned it, but in her great wisdom she gave it to me instead! I'm sure it's a form of torture.

It's now seven a.m. on Sunday morning. The damned thing is ringing and ringing and I can't turn it off. I grabbed it, wrapped it in my shirt and stuffed it under the bed-clothes. It was still ringing its head off, but you know what? The vibration was surprisingly pleasant.

Just when I was getting ready to enjoy it, the damned thing stopped. Utter silence! But oh, what bliss! There I was, stretched out like some big, lazy dog with a belly full of best tripe. The curtains were shut; there was no one about. I could dream and laze, and there was not a soul in the whole wide world to disturb me.

'BEN!' It was my darling mother. 'BEN, CAN YOU HEAR ME? GET YOUR LAZY ASS OUT OF THAT BED! IT'S NINE O' CLOCK. TIME FOR SUNDAY MASS!'

'I'M NOT GOING!'

'WHY NOT?'

'I'M SICK!'

'DON'T GIVE ME THAT! I KNOW YOUR LITTLE GAME. YOU'VE NEVER LIKED GOING TO CHURCH, EVEN WHEN YOU WERE A LITTLE BOY!'

'YOU DON'T UNDERSTAND!' I was not going to let her win this time. 'I REALLY AM ILL. I'VE BEEN UP HALF THE NIGHT, BRINGING UP MY DINNER.'

The bedroom door was flung open and there she was, in all her glory: black hat, long black coat and looking for all the world like Darth Vader. 'So, you're ill are you?' Gawd! She's in my bedroom! Was there no peace in this crazy world?

'Oh, Mam, leave me alone … I need my sleep.' I groaned.

'Is that so?' She walked across the room and stood by my bed. It's Hammer Horror all over again.

'So you need your sleep, do you?' She said quietly.

'Yes, please.' Am I pathetic or what?

'So, you've been throwing up, have you?' Even quieter.

'Honestly, Mum, it was awful. Look, it might be best if you go without me. Let me get my rest, eh?' Groaning, I slid under the covers. 'I hurt all over, I really do.'

'Do you now?' Oh, God! I thought, She's folded her arms. When my mother folds her arms, it's war.

'Please, Mum. I'll make up for it next Sunday.' I'm a past master at grovelling. 'Next week, I promise to be up and dressed before you even come down for breakfast.'

'So, you've had no sleep, you've been sick, and you hurt

all over?' She drew back the covers and looked me in the eye (it felt like my last moment on earth). 'Is that the honest truth, Ben?'

'Well of course it is! Do you think I'm making it all up?' (One Christmas, I played Joseph at school; the drama teacher swore I had a future in acting.) 'Ooh, Mum, I feel terrible.'

I gave a rending groan and made a face like a stripped kipper. Shameful I know, but when confronted by the enemy, what can a man do?

'Now, I'm not calling you a liar, son, but I can't understand it.' Mum had a look in her eye I didn't like.

'Why not?'

'Because your poor father was ill most of the night with shocking wind. I had to get out of the room or faint from the smell. Anyway, I thought he might have woken you, what with all the noise and such. But you were so deep asleep, I didn't have the heart to wake you.'

'Shh, well … you see…' (She was on to me.) 'I must have just got back into bed…' Give it up, Ben, I told myself. It's too late; you've been well and truly rumbled.

Her tight little face stretched into a sly, knowing smile that would frighten elephants. 'You must be feeling better now,' she said, 'I'll see you downstairs in ten minutes.'

'I'M NOT GOING!' That told her.

'TEN MINUTES, BEN!' That told me!

'I'VE ALREADY SAID … I AM NOT GOING, AND

54

THAT'S FINAL.' End of! Not up for negotiation! Last word on the subject.

With her good and told, and out of my hair, I sighed, and cuddled up with my Big Ted.

I've done it! At long last I've put my foot down; both at home and at work, and not before time neither.

What's more, although I might live to regret it, I have definitely decided to broach the matter of sharing a flat with Dickie Manse brains-in-his-pants. Though it will mean I'll have to take on his hairy mongrel, whose wind problem is almost as frightening as my father's.

The day seemed to have ended as well as expected.

The church was cold as usual. I warbled through two hymns I'd never even heard of, but when the organ struck up *All Things Bright and Beautiful*, I sang my heart out with the best of them.

The collection box got me on the way out. I only had two pence, which I threw in with a grand gesture. 'Thank you, sir,' the verger tucked the coin back into my hand, 'I think you need it more than we do.' I was miffed. What real man wears a *skirt* anyway!

As I slunk out, I felt a sharp pinch on the back of my leg. 'You're a mean bugger, you are!'

If he wasn't just three feet high, and sucking a sticky dummy, I might have smacked him one. (Though I did manage to stamp craftily on his foot. It did my heart good to see the shock on his little pink face.)

Ah well, happy days. Tomorrow *has* to be an improvement.
Doesn't it?

BEDFORD
OCTOBER, SATURDAY

Well here we are, diary. After all the doubts and aggravation, today's the day, and I really hope I'm not about to make the biggest mistake of my entire life (though, Lord knows, I've made enough mistakes already to sink a battleship!).

I'm sitting on the edge of my bed, with my head in hands and all my pitiful worldly possessions lying round me, consisting of: four pairs of plain brown socks, two ties – one formal for unexpected events, and one bright green with a motif of Donald Duck in the corner. Then there are seven pairs of yellow and blue spotted underpants from Marks and Sparks (Laura bought me those two weeks before she threw me out – is it any wonder our sex life took a nosedive!).

Fraying at the elbow, my black Travolta bomber jacket was lying crumpled on the floor; beside it was a blue windjammer depicting a skier in action; there are my favourite baggy jeans; two pairs of serviceable trousers for work, and my one and only suit for unexpected formal events (which so far number two in total – one was for an aunt's funeral, and the other ever ready for when the virtual owner of the kennels pays a flying visit, to check that his business is not being run into the ground).

Then there are the usual man's things, like a baseball cap, an unused cricket bat, a pair of dodgy sunglasses from House of Fraser, oh and a packet of extra-size condoms for unexpected emergencies (also never used – how pitiful is that?).

'How can you be so ungrateful?' The door was flung open and there she was – every sane man's worst nightmare! 'I hope you know you're breaking my heart.'

'Oh, Mam! Don't start all that again!' Her eyes were red-raw from crying, and she was wringing her hands together like she had my neck between them. 'It's no use, Mum.' Oh yes, I can be heartless when tried, 'I'm leaving and that's that!' Before she could persuade me to stay, I began throwing my things into a bag like the ship was going down!

'Oh, Ben, after what I've done for you, I honestly don't know how you can up and away like this.' She was so close I could feel the fire of her breath down the back of my shirt collar. 'I took you in when that witch of a wife threw you out. I've loved you and cherished you. I've washed your dirty socks and made sure you never go to work without your lunch pack, and when you had the flu, I sat by you day and night and held your hand. I'm your mother, for heaven's sake. You can't leave me here with your dad!'

A huge surge of compassion made me forget all the bad things, 'Aw, Mum, I'm sorry, I really am. I know you sat with me when I was ill, and I know you washed my dirty socks, and I'll always be grateful to you for taking me back when I had nowhere else to go. And you will never know what it meant to me when you lovingly packed my lunch.'

I tried not to let her see how badly my life had been affected by these things, 'I promise you this, Mum ... if I live to be a hundred I will never forget what you did.'

'There you are, y'see!' (She was so puffed with pride I hadn't the heart to burst her bubble.) 'Nobody can say I haven't been a model mother.'

Drawing myself up to my full height, I placed my hands tenderly on her lardy shoulders, and smiling into her pea-like eyes, I tried to soften the blow of my imminent departure. 'Look, Mum, I know it's hard for you ... oh, and me of course. But I'm not a little boy any more. It's time I moved on ... don't you think?'

I swear to God I didn't see it coming. She smiled at me, then before I could scream for help, she had me against the wall, her hands at my throat, 'YOU'RE NOT GOING ANYWHERE!' I could have yelled for my father, but something told me he was probably lying downstairs with his head caved in.

'Let go of me!' I gurgled, (though it wasn't easy with her

59

shovel-like hands flattening my windpipe). 'I promise ... I'll come back and visit!'

'Oh, no you don't! I'm not falling for that old lie! (When she smiled that smile, I knew I had to escape or die.) 'You're a liar, just like your useless father. You say you'll come back and visit, but I know you won't! I'm sorry, Ben. I did not want it to come to this, but you have to understand. Y'see you are my one and only child, and I can never allow you to leave this house.'

She waggled a key in front of my face, 'I would not be doing my duty as a mother, if I let you leave! You're too vulnerable. People take advantage of you. Look at the way Laura treated you! And look at that slip of a girl ... what's her name ... Poppy? One of these fine days she'll have the pants off you and there'll be a child on the way, you see if I'm not right. Then she'll leave you and I'll have to pick up the pieces as usual. Oh, and what about this new idiot you seem to be hanging around with ... what's his name ... oh, yes, Dickie Manse brains-in-his-pants. And why would a man get a nickname like that, eh?' (When she winked one eye like that, she had a distinct look of Captain Pugwash.)

Suddenly the sound of Dad's voice calling her made her lose her grip and that was my chance, which I took like a true hero. 'You come back here!' she yelled as I grabbed my bag and ran. 'I haven't finished with you yet.' As I half ran half fell down the stairs she was right behind me; it was like being trapped at the foot of an avalanche, like any minute she would fall on top of me and I'd never be seen again.

'Leave me alone, Mum!' The terror must have been etched on my face, because when I got to the bottom of the stairs my father leaped aside, shouting, 'KEEP GOING, SON ... IF YOU DON'T GET OUT NOW, YOU NEVER WILL!'

As I ran out the door, my bag fell open and all my underpants fell out on to the pavement. 'Somebody's got a colourful ass, that's for sure!' That was grumpy old Bob from the corner house. Judging from his long, straggly beard and dirty overcoat, I wouldn't be surprised if his underpants have never seen the light of day. (That's if he wears any. Ooh! What a frightful image!)

'RUN FOR YOUR LIFE, SON!' That was Dad. 'YOU'RE FREE! FREE!'

He stopped yelling when mother wrapped him round the head with her fist. 'GO ON THEN!' she yelled at me as I fled, 'YOU'LL MAKE A MESS OF THINGS LIKE YOU ALWAYS DO, AND THEN YOU'LL COME CRAWLING BACK, YOU SEE IF I'M NOT RIGHT!'

Panicking, I almost ran head on into Dickie Manse brains-in-his-pants as he came rushing round the corner. 'Whoa there!' He blocked my path. 'I was coming to fetch you. We're supposed to have picked up the key to our new pad half an hour ago.'

'BEN! DON'T TAKE ANY NOTICE OF THAT WEIRDO. COME BACK HERE THIS MINUTE!'

'Crikey, what's got into her?' Dickie Manse brains-in-his-pants peered down the street at the mad marauder, 'She looks like Cruella de Vil ... you know, her in that film ... with the spotty dogs and all that.'

'RUN FOR IT, MANSEY...' I grabbed him and took off. 'QUICK ... IF YOU VALUE YOUR BLOCK AND TACKLE.' (I know how fond he is of fishing ... for girls that is.)

We set off at a run, with mother's voice following us to the bitter end, 'THAT'S IT ... CLEAR OFF THEN ... YOU AND YOUR HALFWIT FRIEND! AND DON'T BLAME ME IF PEOPLE CALL YOU A COUPLE OF LAYS!' The eerie sound was her gardening trowel as it whistled past my ear and impaled itself in Maggie Leatherhead's front door.

When we got clear, Dickie Manse brains-in-his-pants had a question (as always).

'What does she mean ... "a couple of lays"?' he puffed.

'Search me!' My mum was a complete mystery.

Behind us my warring parents could be heard screaming at each other. 'WHAT THE DEVIL WAS THAT YOU CALLED 'EM?' I'm proud of my dad.

'WHAT D'YOU MEAN, YOU SILLY OLD FOOL?' Mother yelled back.

'YOU SAID PEOPLE WILL CALL THEM "A COUPLE OF LAYS".'

'SO WHAT IF I DID?'

'BUT WHAT DOES IT MEAN?'

'YOU KNOW VERY WELL WHAT IT MEANS!'

'I WOULDN'T ASK IF I KNEW.'

'IT MEANS MEN WHO PREFER THE COMPANY OF MEN ... IF YOU UNDERSTAND MY MEANING?'

'YOU DITHERING IDIOT! THAT'S *"GAYS"*... NOT "LAYS"!'.

It got me thinking, 'Hey, I hope you're not getting any ideas about you and me?' I asked Dickie Manse brains-in-his-pants, 'I mean, I for one, have no particular leanings in that direction.'

Dickie laughed out loud, 'Well, neither have I,' he said with a wink, 'you should know by now ... I'm more partial to peaches and cream than meat and two veg...' He slid his arm through mine, 'But I'm an adventurous guy ... up for anything, if you take my meaning?'

Giving him an almighty shove, I widened the distance between us, 'TAKE YOUR HANDS OFF ME!'

Undeterred, he suggested with a twinkle in his eye, 'I reckon we'd best get this flat organised ... after all, we're free souls now aren't we?' I did not like the look in his eye. 'There'll be nobody to tell us what to do, or how to behave.'

There was a tense moment before he started laughing, and I realised he was having me on.

'Did you pick up the keys?' I asked.

'O' course.' Dickie looked very pleased with himself.

'Good!' At last! Something was going right for once.

Our laughter rang through the streets as we made our

way to the fish and chip shop. 'I reckon we'll be all right, you and me,' Dickie said encouragingly.

It took him a full ten minutes to get the door open, 'Get away, I can do it,' he argued when I asked to have a go. 'I'm not so stupid I can't turn a key in the lock!'

Eventually the key turned and the door was flung open, 'We're in!'

As we climbed the stairs to the flat above, every wooden step groaned and shifted, and I began to wonder if we'd ever get down again. 'We'll soon have this place shipshape,' announced Dickie Manse brains-in-his-pants. 'Now that we're free men with nobody to nag and control us, there is nothing we can't do!'

All the same, when we flung open the top door to the stench of dead birds and damp, not to mention the holes in the walls, I couldn't help but wonder if I'd bitten off more than I can chew.

'We'll turn this place round, you see if we don't!' Grabbing a black sack that had been used to stuff a hole under the window-sill, Dickie was in there like a madman, collecting all the stiff, black crows that had obviously got in down the chimney and never managed to get out again.

'You won't regret going in with me,' he said cockily. 'It'll be great! Parties every night … Girls! Let me at 'em!'

When I gave no answer, he turned round, disappointed at my long face, 'What's up?'

64

'It stinks in here.'

'Well, that's because of the crows. But look, they're all in the bag now.'

'It still stinks.'

'That's because the damp is coming in through the holes in the plaster, and that tight git downstairs is too busy making money from his chip shop to spend the necessary on this place.'

He slapped me on the shoulder, leaving sticky bits of feathers on my windjammer. 'Come on, Ben! It'll be great, honest. The landlord said we could make improvements! We can get everything we need from the DIY place in King Street, and once we've rolled up our sleeves and got stuck in you won't recognise this place.

'You really think it'll be all right, do you?' I asked.

'Absolutely, yes!' At least Dickie had the right attitude.

'And you don't think I was too hard on my mum … running out like that, and not saying cheerio properly?' I still wasn't sure if I'd done the right thing.

'Tell me this, Ben … if you hadn't run out on here, what would she have done?' Dickie wanted to know.

'Probably locked me in the cellar and fed me on bread and water.'

'There you have it, then. With people like your mother, slightly unhinged and controlling, a man has no choice but to make a run for it.' He gave me one of those looks that panicked me, 'Do you agree?'

I nodded, which instantly earned me a hearty pat on the back. 'Good man! Now then … let's explore the rest of this wonderful place!' And off he went, totally convinced that this dirty, stinky hellhole was the answer to our prayers.

I'm not sure of anything any more.

But it's too late now, and there's no turning back.

Rightly or wrongly, I have burned my bridges with a vengeance.

Heaven help me!

BEDFORD
NOVEMBER, SUNDAY

Well, diary, it's been a while since me and Dickie Manse brains-in-his-pants moved in over the fish and chip shop, and I've been so busy, this is the first time I've been able to get to my diary.

The first night we stayed in the flat was so terrifying, I'll remember it to the end of my days (and if we don't soon solve the problem of these big old crows trying to break in, the end will be sooner than we think!). I remember my dad fishing out an old recording of Hitchcock's thriller, *The Birds*, and y'know what, I reckon me and Dickie Manse brains-in-his-pants have landed right in the middle of it!

Just now I nearly leaped out of my skin when he popped his head round my bedroom door. 'I don't believe it!' he gawped, 'It's gone eight, and there's you, still lying in bed. Oh and what's that you're scribbling?'

'Nothing!' I rammed the diary and pen under the bed-clothes with such force I nearly did myself a private injury; not that anyone would notice what with my social life being non-existent. 'Anyway, what's the problem?' I grumbled. 'After all the work we did yesterday, I deserve a lie in.'

He threw himself on the bed, his face wreathed in one of them obnoxious grins. 'Don't tell me you keep a diary?' he laughed. 'Only prissies and young girls keep a diary!'

I gave him a forceful push, 'As you well know, I am neither a prissie *nor* a young girl. And if you don't mind, I'd like you to clear off while I get washed and dressed!'

'I'm not going, not till you show me what you're hiding under the bedclothes.'

'I mean it,' I had to be forceful, 'I want you to bugger off, out of my room!'

'Not until I see what you've got there.'

'I've got nothing that might interest you, so you either leave of your own accord, or I throw you out.'

'Ooooh!' Again, that obnoxious grin. 'Touchy touchy, Ben!' When he made a grab for the bedclothes, I gave him an almighty shove that sent him sprawling across the room. He scrambled up and glared at me. 'You've really hurt my feelings!' he muttered. 'I've seen a side to you that's positively awful!'

Feeling guilty, I waited for him to leave, then I leaped out of bed, locked my door, and hid the diary under a loose floorboard. I then ran to the grubby old bathroom, had a quick swill, combed my hair, had a shave and got dressed.

When I walked into the makeshift kitchen, the delicious aroma of sizzling bacon drifted across the room. 'I made breakfast,' Dickie said sullenly. 'You can eat it or leave it, I don't care!' He sulkily slid two plates on to the table, each loaded with mushrooms, bacon and egg, and even a slice of toast on the side (it was burned black, but I didn't complain. After all, I needed him to help me paint the flat).

An hour later, we set off in Dickie Manse's old banger. 'I hate this useless heap!' he kept saying, 'I *really* hate it!'

'So, why didn't you keep your old Audi?'

'You know why. Because I've been put on short time, and I would never have been able to pay my half deposit for the flat, let alone help with all the paint and brushes and new plaster for that gaping hole in the ceiling…'

'Which I might add, *you* put there yourself, when you were putting things in the loft and fell through the ceiling … *twice*!'

'Well there you go!' Like many before it, the conversation was fast developing into a full blown row, 'If *you'd* gone up there like I asked you, the ceiling might still be intact. You know I have a fear of heights.'

'A fear of work you mean!'

'I'll ignore that! Anyway, this flat needs a fortune spending on it. If we wait for the landlord to do it, it'll be ages before we can invite anyone back. We both know that sacrifices have to be made.'

'All right, I get the picture,' I apologised. 'Sorry.'

'No, it's me that should be sorry. I'm just accident prone. I can't seem to help myself.'

'You need to calm down,' I reminded him. 'What about the other day, when you leaped out of the car and had a real go at the man in front, because he didn't move forward when the lights turned to green?'

'Too damned right! He deserved a telling off!'

'No he didn't. The poor sod had broken down. He couldn't move even if he wanted to.'

'That's not the point!' Dickie was a genius at arguing. 'There's a code on the roads, and we all have to follow it.'

'What code?' Sometimes, he's a mystery unto himself.

'Like I told him … the lights go red, and you *stop*! The lights go green, and you *go*!'

'But he couldn't *go*!'

'That's what I'm saying. He couldn't go when he should have done. So he held everybody up and no doubt they all arrived at work stressed out.'

When Dickie Manse gets some silly idea in his head, there is just no reasoning with him. So I gave up while the going was good.

Ten minutes later, we were circling the roundabout outside the B&Q store, when the car gave a loud snort and shuddered to a halt. 'Oh no!' It was the last thing we needed. 'The damned engine's conked out!' Now it was *my* turn to panic.

'We don't know that yet,' Dickie said. 'Let's not panic until we know what the problem is.' Dickie got out of the car and peeped under the bonnet. 'It's well heated up,' he said, climbing back inside, 'have you got your mobile with you?'

'Yes, why?' I asked suspiciously.

'Because I haven't got one now. You know very well I sold it, so we could get new door locks.' Dickie was getting sulky.

'If you hadn't made that agreement with the landlord *he'd* have bought the door locks! Never mind that. What do we do now?'

Dickie thrust a card under my nose, 'Ring these people,' he instructed, 'they're sure to come out and help us.'

I was duly impressed, 'Aha! So you got that emergency cover after all. About time too!' I'd been nagging him to cover himself and the car in case of a breakdown.

'Ben! Will you please stop nattering and get on with it, while I see what I can do.'

'Do you want me to have a look?' I needed to feel useful.

He gave me one of those shrinking looks. 'Not one of your best ideas,' he quipped, 'seeing as how you're like a light gone out where engines are concerned!'

While he scrambled out of the car, I read the card. It said:

If it hadn't been so tragic, it might have been funny. 'DICKIE BLOODY MANSE ... GET BACK HERE, DAMMIT!'

He looked up, 'Are they on their way?' he asked, all covered in muck and oil. 'Did you tell them it was urgent? How long will they be?'

'They're not coming.' I was seething.

'And why's that?' Dickie looked puzzled.

'Because they're not car people, and they don't do emergency breakdowns.'

'Rubbish! They gave me their card ... any problem they said ... just give us a call.'

'You're a prat, and you always will be!'

'Oh, just give it here! I can't even trust you to make a simple call.' Grabbing the card from my hands he glanced at it and flung it back, 'You're the prat!' he said righteously. 'Look! It says right there, NO JOB TOO BIG OR SMALL – ALL YOU HAVE TO DO IS CALL.'

'You're absolutely right,' I had to agree, 'the only thing is … they're *gardeners*, not mechanics. That means they tend to plants, *not cars or lorries*, or even pushbikes … but *plants*, as in tulips, or forget-me-nots.'

'So are you saying they lied?' He's either thick or away with the fairies!

'No. I am *not* saying they lied. What I'm saying is you must have leapt to the wrong conclusion. Now we're stuck at the roundabout, with cars jammed up behind us and a thousand hooters playing a tune. So, to my mind, there is only one thing to do.'

'And what's that?'

'We'll have to push this heap of junk off the road. I'll ring Poppy and ask if she knows any mechanics. Failing that, we'll have to find one ourselves.'

Dickie was adamant, 'You won't catch me pushing this thing. I've got my back to think of … never mind my reputation.'

The queue of irritated, red-faced drivers watched as we pushed that sorry heap of metal to the side of the road, and as they went by it was fingers in the air and looks that could kill … and that was just Dickie Manse brains-in-his-pants.

'Behave yourself.' I told him, but as always he took no notice.

'Now what do we do?' Leaning over the bonnet, panting and puffing, he did look a poor and sorry thing.

Someone had to keep it together, so I squared my shoulders and made a plan. 'Look, I'll ring Poppy like I said. For now we'll just go inside and buy the paint and ceiling plaster, and all the other stuff we came for.'

'How can I?' he wailed. 'We've no way of getting the stuff back to the flat.'

'We'll arrange for delivery.' How cunning is that?

'And who's gonna pay the fifteen quid delivery charge?'

I gave him a helping hand towards the main doors, 'I'll pay the charge.' Magnanimous to the end, that's me.

With hunched shoulders and a pug-face, he made straight for the paint racks, 'Look! They've got a selection of orange,' he grinned, pointing to the top shelf.

Panic set in, 'Are you sure it's orange you want?' I asked hopefully. 'If I were you, I'd go for a quieter colour.'

'Well, you're not me. *You* choose the colour you want for *your* room, and I'll choose the colour *I* want. Orange is a bright, happy colour.'

There was no changing his mind.

Thankfully, I was far enough away when it happened. Dickie climbed on to the bottom shelf to reach up and grab the particular shade of orange he wanted, then the whole thing unfolded like some creeping nightmare. Firstly the bottom shelf he was standing on collapsed, then all four shelves came down like a crumbling pack of cards, while underneath it all was Dickie Manse brains-in-his-pants making a run for it, screaming and yelling like a banshee. The top shelf fell from the farthest end and got him good, with pots of paint spewing out in all directions.

When it was over, the ensuing silence was broken only by the shouts of assistants trying to bring order through chaos.

Wide-eyed and groaning, Dickie was lying on the ground, well and truly tangoed from top to bottom. 'Help me,' he groaned, winking at me through one splattered eye and looking like some deranged monster from *Star Trek*. 'Don't stand there gawping at me … get me up!'

After a telling off, a hefty bill and a quick hose down by two burly security guards, Dickie was marched off the premises and me with him.

On the way back to the flat, he talked of nothing but the two security guards, 'I might go back and have a word with them tomorrow,' he said. 'It's only right that I go and apologise.'

While he chatted, he kept his thumb permanently in the air begging a lift, but no one stopped. Instead they laughed and jeered and probably hurried home to tell their folks about this lunatic on the roads.

I did feel sorry for him though.

I felt sorry for myself too. What have I let myself in for?

We've only really started getting the flat together. The landlord, Antonio, is a big, wobbly shape of a man but harmless enough. His wife, Maria, is another story … she's a big, bosomy woman with all the fire and anger of an Italian momma. Once we'd stupidly agreed to do the work on the flat, she told us we had to get it looking beautiful, or we'd be out on our ear. That's fine by me, because I have no wish to live in a pigsty. The plumber is coming next week to fit a new loo, and that's only the start.

After what's happened today though, I can't help but wonder what new disasters await us.

My dad's been to see us once, but I haven't seen hide nor hair of my mother.

You know when the hairs on the back of your neck stand up and you're filled with a feeling of dread? Well, that's how I'm beginning to feel.

It's back to work on Monday, and no one will be more pleased than me.

BEDFORD
NOVEMBER, SATURDAY

SETTLING IN ...

'**B**en! Did you hear what I said?' Eager to leave, Dickie Manse was leaning against the open door with his hand on the door knob. 'Ben! Have you gone deaf or what?'

'No, but I will if you don't stop yelling!' I ought to be giving him a piece of my mind, not the other way round; but would he even take the slightest notice? No, he would not! The thing is ... wouldn't we *all* like to have a night out on the town? Wouldn't we *all* like to leave our dirty dishes in the sink for somebody else to wash up? And what about the flat, and the painting, and the cleaning up? Who's left to do all that? Why muggins here, who else!

'Are you in a mood with me?' There he goes again, playing the victim.

'Why? D'you think I have reason to be in a mood with you?'

'None so far as I can see. No.'

'Then you can't see very far then, can you?'

'Aw, look, Ben. I know I said I'd stay in and help with the painting an' all. But I've changed my mind. I mean ... I can change my mind if I want to, can't I?'

'Oh, absolutely!' How could he be so damned insensitive? How could he live in a pigsty like this and not want to do something about it?

I let him have it, 'You get off and enjoy yourself,' I told him. 'Never mind if the place reeks of booze and ciggies, and the coffee spills all over the floor and bits of rotting food under the rug.'

I was really getting going now, 'Oh, and don't worry about the rats that will soon find their way in, thinking it's free nosh and boarding; and who incidentally could well find their way into your bed and bite your no-good arse! Just get off and have a good time. Don't give me a second thought. Well? Go on then, what are you hanging about for?'

'Aw, come on, Ben ... I really want you to come with me.' Has he even heard a single word I've said?

'Why don't you leave it all till next week, Ben,' he wailed. 'It's Saturday night for pity's sake! We're a couple of single blokes. We've been working all week, and we have a right to enjoy ourselves ... find some stunning-looking girls... have a bit of a flirt and that. We might even play a game of pool and afterwards we can bring the girls back here. Oh, come on, Ben! What do you say?'

God! Is he thick or what? Why ever did I let myself be talked into sharing a flat with him? My mother said it would end in disaster and I'm beginning to think she was right. Mind you, it was a good idea and it might *still* work out okay, if only Dickie Manse brains-in-his-pants could be persuaded to do his fair share.

Instead, he was still going on about leaving the place looking like a tip, to go out and enjoy ourselves, and even after we talked it all over (for the umpteenth time) and agreed to stay in and spend the whole weekend painting the flat right through.

I should have known he'd change his mind ... again! It didn't take me long to discover that he's a lazy, good for nothing, useless git!

Well okay! If that's what he wants, he might as well clear off. I'll just carry on sorting out my paint pots and brushes, like I planned.

To tell the truth, I wouldn't have minded a night out; in fact I had an earlier offer, but I turned her down, because me and lazy bones had said this was the weekend when we would tidy up and paint the flat.

Okay, so the offer of going out with a girl wasn't such a big deal, as it came from Poppy, and I'm not altogether destroyed by not taking her to the cinema. Though I must say, I felt like a louse telling her I couldn't go after all.

When she started crying, alarm bells rang. I mean, it's a well known fact that she's always had a crush on me, but it's never been more than that and I can live with it if I have to. Just lately though, she's started following me everywhere. She peeks at me round corners and rushes to get me a cuppa when I arrive in the morning, and the other day when she brought that puppy in for me to examine, she kept touching me with the tip of her fingers. I'm not shy, but it was nerve wracking!

Oh yes, I can see I'm gonna have to watch Poppy, or she'll get the idea that I fancy her. Come to think of it, choosing to decorate the flat instead of taking her to the cinema might be a blessing in disguise. Good grief! She's just a kid. I've no idea why she thinks I fancy her. I haven't given her any encouragement; well, I mean, if I have, I never meant to. All the same, I probably would have taken her to the cinema because there's no harm in that, but Dickie Manse brains-in-his-pants put a stop to that, and now the miserable git has gone against his word.

'Right then, if you're not coming, I'll be off. See you later, eh?'

'Fine. Cheerio. Enjoy yourself!'

'Right then, I will!'

'Go on then!' I had to get the last dig in, 'Don't waste precious time talking to me. I've got work to do ... or have you forgotten?'

'Leave it out, Ben!'

'Well, go on then. Let me get on. If I don't get stuck into the painting now, it'll never get done.'

'It *will*, I promise!' He took a step into the room, a forlorn look on his face. 'I've already told you, I'll help you, but not tonight. I'm due a night out, and so are you. Let the painting wait. There's only the kitchen and the bathroom left to do. It won't take long if we both get stuck in.' He looked like a kid who'd had his ice cream snatched away.

'You're right!' And he was. 'We *are* due a night out. Like we said last week and the week before, and the week before that ... let the painting wait, and the dirt and the dust and the stink ... let it all fester while we go out and enjoy ourselves. Oh, and let's not take any notice of Antonio from the chip shop downstairs, who incidentally threatened to call out the health and safety officer. Why should we worry about the fact that the beer from an over-turned bottle dripped through the floorboards, straight into his chip pan and ruined all his fishcakes? Who is he anyway ... only the bloody landlord, that's who!'

There was a long moment of complete silence. 'I know why you're in a mood, Ben. It's because Poppy's got the hots for you, and you really like her but you don't know how to handle it. Yes! That's the truth, and now you're taking it out on me.'

I shook my head in disgust. 'Instead of talking rubbish, take a look around you! Just look at this place ... it's a dung heap!' There were two empty wine bottles on the window-sill, cigarette butts ground into the floorboards, a mangled pile of dirty jeans in one corner, a cup of coffee from the previous night spilled near the chair where Dickie Manse brains-in-his-pants had been stretched out snoring like a rhino, and most of our belongings were still in boxes, which were littered in every room, right round the flat. There was even a pair of his manky shorts hanging on the door knob!

'This place is disgusting!' I told him. 'It's not much better than when we first moved in. In fact, in some ways it's *worse*!'

'All right, so it's not good,' Dickie Manse had to agree, 'but there's no rule to say we can't still enjoy ourselves. We can spend all day tomorrow clearing it up, and then make a start on the painting afterwards. I'll help you. I really will.'

I was not falling for his lies again. 'Look … I'll stay in and set to work,' I ended the argument. 'When the flat is painted from top to bottom, and we've sorted out all our things … then we can think about a social life.'

'Party pooper!'

'There's nothing I'd rather do tonight than have a good time. But it's not going to happen, because tonight I'm doing what I said I would do. So let that be an end to it!'

'Okay!' Sulking like a ten year old, Dickie Manse was well and truly miffed. 'That's fine by me, but don't ask me to give up my Saturday night, because I mean to go out, find me a girl, and have the time of my life.'

Suddenly I had this awful, familiar feeling in the pit of my stomach, which told me that disaster was only minutes away.

Lolling against the door, Dickie gave a parting wink. 'I'm a free soul,' he declared. 'Free as the wind! I can do what I like! Oh yes!'

Leaping up he gave a little kick of the heels, lost his balance, fell through the open door and went skidding on his rear, all the way down the stairs, screaming like a madman at every bump and tumble.

Then there was an eerie, deafening silence.

'Dickie! Are you all right?' Peering over the bannister, I was shocked to see him all crumpled and twisted.

'Help me!' he groaned.

Thinking he'd busted every bone in his body, I ran down the stairs two at a time.

'I've broken my back ... ooh ... help me, Ben. I'm done for, I know it! No, don't lie to me,' his sorry eyes looked up, 'this is it, Ben. I'm finished.'

I assured him he wasn't finished and with a strength I didn't even know I had, I managed to half lift, half drag him up the stairs and into his bedroom, where I threw him on the bed and flopped down beside him. 'It's *me* that's finished,' I gasped. 'I reckon I'm about to have a heart attack.'

Realising his ankle was beginning to swell like a balloon, I managed to lay Dickie out flat on the bed. 'Don't move!' I told him. 'I'm ringing the doctor.'

It was like a military operation, with Dickie Manse brains-in-his-pants, threatening me with all kinds of retribution. 'I'm not having no doctor touch me!' he yelled. 'I mean it! Don't you dare call a doctor!'

Being Saturday, I called the hospital. When I got through to a doctor I explained the situation. 'I don't think there's anything broken ... but he's in a lot of pain, and his ankle is swelling up fast.'

There was a pause while I listened to the doctor's instructions, and all the time Dickie Manse was in my ear. 'What's he saying? Tell him there's been a mistake and I don't need him.' He tried to get off the bed and ended up draped over the radiator.

'Yes, doctor, I'll do that.' By now I was beginning to panic, 'Hang on a minute please ... don't go away.'

I went to do as the doctor instructed. 'Leave me be!' By now, Dickie Manse had laid himself out on the floor and was having none of it. 'Get off! Ouch! Bloody hell! Are you trying to kill me or what?'

'Shut up, you big baby! I'm only doing what the doctor told me to.'

I went back to the phone, 'Are you still there ... doctor, hello...'

'The bugger's gone, hasn't he? They're all the same ... they take their massive wages and run at the first sign of work!' There was no shutting him up. 'He's left me here to die, hasn't he? What's this country coming to, that's what I'd like to know?'

'For pity's sake will you shut up! No, not you doctor, it's *him*. The patient. He's frightened I think. Oh no, he's a grown man ... at least his body is, but I don't know about his brain. Yes, you're right, he is a bit of a softie, yès ... I did what you said, and he can bend his knee, and his ankle moves but it's terribly painful; in fact he almost bit off my ear when I twisted his leg about. Oh no, I don't *think* he's having a fit, but I don't suppose we'll ever know, will we? No, it's not bleeding, but it's that swollen it looks like a leg of pork. Okay, doctor. Thank you. Yes, I'll do that.'

'Is he sending an ambulance for me?' Dickie groaned.

''Fraid not.'

'Well there you are, it's exactly what I said ... he's given up on me ... leaving me here to die, that's his little game, isn't it, eh?'

Now he was on his soapbox, 'A fat wage packet, a house on the hill ... three weeks in Blackpool and they still can't tend the sick! But what do they care, tell me that? I'll just be one more casualty ... drop him in the ground, give his crutch to the next man and let that be an end to him. That's the attitude!'

I let him rant and rave and scream and holler, until we were downstairs, inside a taxi and on the way to Bedford hospital.

'I'm not staying.' He was still on the rampage, 'You can tell them. I am definitely not staying in there for them to have their wicked way with me.'

'What ... you mean the nurses?'

'No, I mean the big burly porters. Oh, yes! I've heard all about it, don't you worry.'

'You're talking rubbish.' What planet does he live on?

'Rubbish is it? Huh! You listen to me, Ben, if I'm wheeled away never to be seen again, it'll be your fault!'

'Will you for pity's sake stop? You won't be staying anyway. They need the beds for the really ill. You're going to Casualty like the doctor said.'

Once there they took him away into a cubicle behind the screens, where he shouted and bawled so much that the toddler next to me started crying that she wanted to go home; and there was no shutting her up. She then wet her pants, and her mother had to take her to the loo. A minute later she came marching out with the girl still in tears, 'What kind of place is this, with no toilet roll in the loo!'

She had a go at the duty nurse, who had obviously had a long day because she let loose with a load of nasty verbal. Another woman intervened, then the husband had his say and a doctor was called. Then there was a fight between two men; one with his arm in a sling and the other on crutches. The little girl wet herself again, and all hell was let loose.

As for me, I kept well out of it.

In the midst of all the chaos, Dickie Manse brains-in-his-pants was patched up and sent away in a wheelchair, with strict instructions to 'Rest the ankle for a few days ... just a bad strain that's all. Certainly not a matter of life or death!'

We made for the waiting room. 'What's going on here?' he asked as a flying object missed him by inches.

'Toilet paper,' I giggled, and started running him across the car park, until a nurse came and retrieved the wheel-chair.

Having left the building, you could have been forgiven for thinking we'd started World War Three with all the shouting and arguing behind us. 'Get me out of here!' Dickie Manse looked really frightened.

'It was *you* who started all the trouble, with your screaming and bawling from the cubicle. We could hear you in the waiting room. Shame on you! That poor little girl thought you were being murdered, and all for the sake of a sprained ankle.'

Later that night, with Dickie tucked up in bed and snoring like a good un, I took myself off to the kitchen, got a bottle of wine out of the fridge and poured myself a drink. Then another, and another, until the world was rosy and I felt as though I could jump off a doll's house.

Instead, I fell across the table, arms stretched out under my head, and there I fell fast asleep.

Even the knowledge that Dickie Manse brains-in-his-pants was snoring so loud the place shook could not wake me from my delicious, dream-like slumber.

Neither did the note that was slipped under the door.

I'm sorry, Ben,

Dickie's dog is out of control, and his parents can't cope. We've had it round at ours, but it tried to wrap itself round your mother's leg. She didn't mind, but it's not a sight I ever want to see again. First thing in the morning I'll drop the dirty dog off.

Dad.

BEDFORD
DECEMBER, TUESDAY

It's been a nightmare at the flat.

Dickie Manse brains-in-his-pants blocked the toilet, after cleaning up his dirty dog's doings with kitchen roll, which he then flushed down the johnny. I threatened to throw both him and the dog (Battersby! What a name!) out on the street if he didn't teach him some manners. The dog's revenge was to pee all over the TV connection and blow it up.

And as if that wasn't enough, I was carrying a tray through to the kitchen when we had a sudden power cut, and I walked straight into the edge of the door. I'm told I was out for a good five minutes; I saw stars all night, and in the morning I slunk off to work sporting a black eye, which had turned technicolor by the time I got there.

There was chuckling and winking all round. 'Ooh! That looks painful!' That was randy Ronnie, our latest recruit.

(Who, incidentally, seems to have taken a real shine to our Poppy.) I shall have to put a stop to that, as flirting round the kennels is strictly forbidden.

The delivery man gave him some advice, 'Poppy would be a great catch for you, but some girls don't like to be rushed … that's a lesson I learned when I was a lad.' Giving a wonky wink, he threw the sacks of dog meal against the wall and went off to suck on his cigarette.

Little Danny saw the black eye as a kind of trophy. 'Well done!' he chuckled, 'That's what I call a shiner!'

I ignored the lot of them. Until I slipped on a patch of dog muck and slid from one end of the office to the other. 'Oh, Ben, I'm sorry, it's my fault!' Red faced and embarrassed, Poppy came rushing in with a plaited-leather leash in one hand and a bucket and mop in the other. (So far she had not noticed the black eye.)

'What's going on?' I demanded. 'That's not the first dollop of whatsit that's been dumped there!'

'It's Peaches.' Poppy had a soft spot for that spoiled-rotten hairy dishcloth. 'It's her favourite spot.'

'I couldn't give a monkey's if it's her favourite spot or not! You know very well … that pampered pooch should not even be in here. Why isn't she locked up?'

'Well, it's just that she's due to be collected today and I was getting her all prettied up when she ran off.'

'Where is she now?'

'She rang to say she was on her way.'

'NO, not the owner, dappy! I'm talking about the wretched mutt!' Okay, I know I should not have called her dappy, but sometimes she drives me to the edge of distraction.

'I'm *really* sorry, Ben. It's just that she ran off and did her dirty before I could catch her, and now she's hiding under the desk and won't come out!'

Poor Poppy, she can't help being a walking disaster.

I wonder if I should ask her to share the flat with me, and send Dickie packing. It would save her from her crazy parents at least.

I don't know them, but there have been rumours, so Mother said. I've always thought there was something not quite right about two people in their forties dressing up as vampires, covered in luminous pink paint and cavorting about the house in the dark.

'I'll clean it all up,' Poppy crawled out from under the desk. 'You sit down. I'll get a wet cloth and wipe your shoes.'

I hopped to the nearest chair, where she pushed me down and set about taking off my shoe.

'Am I forgiven?' She peered up at me with those soulful blue eyes.

'You'll not be forgiven until you've found that damned dog and got it off the premises, and the owner with it.' I know that sounds heartless, but I am the boss after all.

'All right, if you're sure you don't need me here with you?' Her pretty eyes shone with hope.

'No. I'm fine, thank you all the same. Besides, the troops need you out there.'

'Oh, do you really think so? For a minute there I thought she was about to cry, but then I realised it was the stink coming from my shoes that was making her eyes water.

'Oh look!' Finally clocking my black eye, she nearly sent me through the roof when she stroked it. 'What did you do? Oh, Ben … it looks so sore. Would you like me to bathe it for you?'

'No! Just go and find that stupid dog.'

It was hard to show authority when you've got a black eye and your shoe is covered in dog muck.

With Poppy gone, I managed to get rid of the dog muck and the stink, and afterwards when I looked in the mirror to see this one-eyed Jack staring back at me, I felt like a real prat!

One thing's for sure. I've got to get a grip on my life. I really must lay down a set of rules or I'm bound to lose control and that would never do. First though, I've got another, more horrifying hurdle to cross, and I'm afraid I might never come out alive.

'You'll have to be brave,' I told the cock-eyed image in the mirror. 'Don't be frightened. Just remain calm and don't say or do anything that might be taken the wrong way.'

I was nervous though. I hadn't seen her in a while and the nearer it got, the more nervous I was becoming. 'And remember to stay near an exit so you can make a quick escape if things get too rough.'

Just thinking about her made it hard for me to breathe. 'After all, you've seen enough of your mother's mad ways to know she could lose it at any minute.'

BEDFORD
JANUARY, THURSDAY

I swear I'll spend the rest of my natural life trying to get Christmas day out of my mind.

The minute my mother opened the front door she was on me, 'Oh, my darling boy … I was so worried you might not turn up. I know I've been awful to you, and I know I should forgive you for leaving me and your dad…' (who was skulking behind her, rolling his eyes and making faces) '…but you must realise, you're all I've got…'

Casting an evil eye at Dad, she then lunged forward, grabbed me by the collar, and yanked me indoors before slamming and bolting the door. 'There … I've got you now!' The look on her face was something akin to Johnny Depp on a bad day.

Beginning to panic, I backed away. 'I can only stay long enough to give you your presents and share a meal with you, and then I have to go.' Isn't it strange how lies just pop into your head when you're shaking with terror? 'Dickie Manse is coming back and we have to crack on with the decorating. Oh, and I need to get back and check on Poppy … she's doing the Christmas day shift at the kennels … yes, and then there's that other thing that I'd almost forgotten…' I could actually hear myself getting more and more desperate.

'Ssh, that's enough!' Pushing me into the kitchen, she tied a pinafore round my waist so tight my chest and backside inflated to double their size. 'You and your father can deal with the turkey, while I set the table. Off you go!'

Waddling to the cooker, she turned off the heat, grabbed the pan of brussels and strained them into the colander, 'I'll leave the roast potatoes in for a while longer…' Her smile was meant to be reassuring, but instead it looked pure evil. 'I don't like them all soft and fluffy,' she whispered menacingly, her beady eyes narrowing to slits, 'I like them hard and brown … so you can hear them crack when you crunch them between your teeth.' Rolling back her lips, she gnashed her teeth together, making a strange whistling noise through her nostrils.

As she slithered away, I instinctively slapped my hands over my private parts. 'Don't be frightened,' Dad said, 'you're safe enough. She's all mouth and no trousers.'

Thank God for that, I thought, and wondered why I had ever let her persuade me that my place was here with family on Christmas day.

I was really on edge. Every time she passed my chair, it sent shivers of terror down my back, because I never knew what she might do. She deliberately terrorised me, saying, 'Oh, I've forgotten to get the salt and pepper out of the cupboard,' and rushed past me, running her nail along my neck as she went. Then she forgot the cranberry sauce, and the stuffing, and last of all, she went for the carving knife. 'It needs to be really sharp, to carve off the legs.'

It was the way she said it, with a smile in her voice and a dark, murderous look in her eyes.

By the end of the first course I was a nervous wreck, so when she suddenly jumped up and made for me, I let out a scream and spilled the gravy all over the tablecloth.

'YOU BAD, *BAD* BOY!' She screamed, pinning my finger to the table with the prongs of her fork. 'Just look at my new tablecloth! I bought it as a special surprise for you. And now you've gone and ruined it. Twenty-five pounds that cost me! Did you do it on purpose, *did you*?'

It was when she started towards me that I ran. 'I've got to go. Poppy can't manage on her own ... bye, Dad ... sorry!'

As I ran down the hallway she was hot on my trail, 'YOU COME BACK HERE!'

'GO ON, SON, I'LL DEAL WITH THIS!' That was Father, 'WHATEVER'S WRONG WITH YOU, WOMAN? LEAVE THE LAD ALONE ... IT'S JUST A CHEAP TATTY

TABLECLOTH … IT'S NOT THE END OF THE WORLD, FOR PITY'S SAKE!'

Poor, brave Dad. When she deliberately yanked up her end of the floor runner and sent him flying through the air, it was a sight that would haunt me forever.

As for me, I'd unbolted the door and was off down the road. I could hear my dad screaming like a banshee, but I was not about to look back, no way José!

The new year brought a new woman into my life, though as always, Dickie Manse brains-in-his-pants put a downer on it, 'NANCY CRUDDLE!' His jaw fell, 'My God, there's not a man this side of London who hasn't licked her lipstick!' He laughed out loud, 'Ooh, you've done it now, Ben! I would not like to be in your shoes if *Laura* finds out.'

'What the devil's it got to do with *her*?'

'Nothing, but you know what she's like … she'll kill you. You and Nancy Cruddle *both*.' He gave an evil snigger. 'I have to admire you though. You certainly know how to live dangerously.'

'You're just jealous, because you still haven't found a woman who would take you on.'

'Ah, that's because I'm more choosy than you. I mean … look at your track record. First you let your wife catch you in bed with that girl; then there was that other girl from Blackpool who fell off her donkey and broke your foot. Then you had a fling with a stripper, until her boyfriend knocked the lights out of you. Oh, yes, and then there's Laura … mad as a hatter and possessed of a killer instinct.' He chuckled, 'Mind you … they do say men pick women like their mothers!'

'All right! All right!' Every word he said was true but I wasn't about to admit it, 'So, I've not been the best judge of character so far, but that doesn't mean to say I've got bad taste. One thing's for sure … I mean to give Nancy Cruddle a chance…'

'Well, *I* wouldn't go out with her.'

'Why not exactly … come on, *why not?*'

'Because I'd be afraid of catching something, that's why not!'

'What? You mean like that something you caught from the girl you met at the bus stop. She picked you up and stripped you clean: wallet, keys, everything but your underpants. The trouble is you've lost your touch. You wouldn't recognise a good woman if you saw one!'

'Take that back!'

'NO!'

'Take that back or I'll set the dog on you.'

'*Set the dog on me!*' I laughed out loud. Battersby was flat out on the sofa, legs open and a look of gormless pleasure on his ugly face. Suddenly he made the loudest, longest trump, filling the room with the foulest stink I have ever encountered.

Me and Dickie Manse looked at each other and ran for the door.

'I hate that dog!' he coughed when we were safely outside.

'Give it to Nancy Cruddle…' I said wickedly, '…her dad owns a burger bar.'

It was good that he chased me out the flat and down the street. We both needed the exercise.

'You know what?' I yelled as I ran.

'What?' He still hadn't forgiven me.

'I reckon we'll have to repaint that room, what with the stench of that lot sticking to it…'

Suddenly all I could hear was one pair of running feet, and they were *mine*.

I stopped, peered back, and there he was, hiding in a shop doorway, crouched low with his head in his hands. You were too hard on him, Ben, I thought guiltily. After all, he's having a bad time with women, while they're after *you* left, right and centre. Too good looking by far, that's what you are.

Wanting to make amends, I went back to him, put my hand on his shaking shoulder and told him sternly, 'Stop that prissy crying. If I said anything to hurt you, I'm really sorry.'

He looked up, his eyes wet with tears, and then he started again. But he wasn't crying, he was laughing – wild, loud laughter that echoed down the street. 'Did you see us two fighting to get out the door?' he screeched. 'Phew! I'd have broken it down if I had to!'

With that frantic image in my mind, even I began to titter. 'I've never heard a dog trump like that before,' I told him.

'I have! He did it once before, and almost blew a hole in Mum's sofa.' Dickie was laughing so hard he could hardly talk, 'I bet Nancy Cruddle could let one off to beat it though!'

I tried hard not to laugh, but it was no good and now the pair of us were screeching and crying.

'CLEAR OFF OUTTA MY SHOP DOORWAY ... YOU'RE FRIGHTENING THE CUSTOMERS!'

The shopkeeper was a big fella, with a face like a punctured pumpkin, 'GO ON THEN! CLEAR ORF OUT OF IT!'

Dragging ourselves up from the ground, we made a hasty retreat. 'Did he *really* almost blow a hole in your mum's sofa?' I couldn't imagine that.

'*Two* actually ... there's one dent at the front of the sofa and another at the back.' He was doubled up and hardly able to speak, 'We're not allowed to talk about it, especially in company!'

Back at the fish and chip shop, we found Antonio out on the pavement.

'Lost something, have you?' I asked.

'No. But I'ma looking.'

'What for?'

'There's a terrible, horrible stinka come up,' he said, holding his nose. 'If I don'ta find where it'sa coming from, they'll shut me down.'

It's just as well he didn't see us falling about with laughter, as we crawled up the stairs.

WHAT A DAY!

And there was more to come.

BEDFORD
MARCH, SATURDAY

Dear diary, I'm beginning to see daylight at last!
Today is the first Saturday of March.

The decorating is all finished, with only a few minor accidents and the one time I had to ring the emergencies for Dickie Manse brains-in-his-pants. I kept telling him not to interfere with the wonky light switch, but would he listen? No he would not. His girlish screams set all the local dogs barking, his hair stood up on end, and his pants were scorched. He's a walking disaster! To hear him screaming you'd have thought he was a goner, but he wasn't badly hurt, due to the fact that he'd just taken the dog-muck out for a walk, and still had his rubber wellies on.

Yesterday we had to buy a new washing machine because he overloaded the old one, which then gave up the ghost and literally collapsed.

'We were lucky they could deliver it this morning.'

Peering out from the back of the machine, I waved my spanner at him, 'And if you hadn't dropped the damned thing on the delivery man's foot, he might have been able to install it, instead of being hauled off to hospital with three broken toes and dented shoes. And now I can't even get this damned thing to work!'

'It's not my fault.'

'So, whose fault is it then?'

'His!'

'And how d'you make *that* out?'

'He should have never let his mate go off early.'

'That was because his mate had a call saying his wife had a scare over her pregnancy and was being rushed to hospital.'

'So, do you think it might have been better if I hadn't offered to help?' Dickie asked.

'Well done, you've got it in one!'

'I had no choice. There was nobody else! Especially as you were having your wicked way with Nancy Cruddle.'

'I'll have you know … I was not having my wicked way with her.'

'What then?'

'We were making plans… *wedding* plans, as if you didn't know.' We were supposed to meet up later tonight, but I'm stuck here aren't I, because thanks to you, I'm landed with the job of plumbing in this damned washing machine!'

'You're made to marry Nancy Cruddle.' Dickie said.

'Hey! Don't start that again, you're as bad as my mother!'

'Yes, well, for once she's right.'

'Don't change the subject. We were talking about you and your latest mishap.'

'What mishap?'

'Crippling the poor delivery man.'

'Not my fault!'

In a way I felt sorry for him, 'Okay, I'm sure you don't create chaos on purpose. But to be honest, I've got no idea what I'm supposed to be doing with this thing.' Truth told, I was beginning to panic, 'There are so many pipes and things … I'm not really sure what goes where.'

'D'you want *me* to have a go?'

'Er … no. Best not, eh?'

'You don't think I'm capable, do you?'

'Well, let's just say, I'm just kinda beginning to fathom it out.' Crikey! Who knows *what* would happen if I let *him* loose on it?

In the short time since we moved into the flat, everything that could go wrong *has* gone wrong! Dickie's already gone through the ceiling twice. Another time he tripped over a loose wire and went flying forwards, and if the window hadn't stopped him, he would have ended up splattered on the pavement.

As it was, he smashed three panes in the window, shattered the frame and cut his arm so badly he had to have fourteen stitches.

For the next half hour I struggled with that wretched

machine, and the harder I tried, the worse it got. 'Look! There's a pipe flapping about!' Dickie Manse screamed. 'The water's shooting all over the place ... get a plumber!'

'Shut up will you!' I was past caring by now. 'Catch the damned thing! Go on! Squeeze the ends together!'

'I can't! It's gone mad!' By now the pipe was flapping about, shooting jets of water all over the place.

Soaked to the skin, I gave him a shove, 'Get out of the way, you're worse than useless! Where's the stopcock?'

'The what?'

'The thing that turns off the water! Where is it?'

'How would I know?'

'Well, I've got no idea at all. Dad always dealt with that kinda thing.'

'Look at it, Ben! There must be some way to turn it off – quick before the water pours through to Antonio's chippy!'

'There!' Stamping on the flailing pipe, I got him to hold it tight while I found some wire to tie it up. But no sooner had I done that, then there was a loud, cracking noise and a long bolt flew out of the back of the machine; then a big nut and a whole collection of washers and stuff.

'Leave it be!' Dickie screamed, 'Get the bloody plumber!'

'Will you stop yelling like a big girl's blouse! Look! Take these!' I slid the nuts and bolts at him, 'And get these down to Antonio ... ask him if he's got anything like that kicking about. And ask him to turn off the mains before we all drown!'

'He won't turn off the mains.'

'Why not?'

'I already told you! He needs the water to wash his potatoes.' In my mind's eye I could see Antonio picking out his earwax, and the sight of his grubby shirt sleeves where he constantly wiped away the sweat was gross. If you ask me, his potatoes weren't *all* that needed washing.

'Get down there and tell him he'll have a flood on his hands if he doesn't turn off the mains! And hurry up!'

While he scurried off, I held it all together the best I could. (It's as well I couldn't see the farce unfolding downstairs.)

Later Dickie told me all about it. He burst in through the chip shop door to find Maggie in a foul mood (nothing new there then).

'Maggie! Where's Antonio?' He shouted.

'He's inna the bathroom and he won'ta come out!' Fat arms across her ample bosom, apparently Maggie shrank him with her stare.

'Get him out! There's a leak under the washing machine and we can't stop it! You need to turn the water off!'

'I no turna the water off!'

'Get a plumber then!'

'I no getta the plumber!'

Dickie then told me he started yelling. Actually, I could hear him from the flat.

'Antonio! Come out ... it's an emergency!'

'He won'ta come out!'

'Why not?'

'Because he very frightened.'

'What's he frightened of?'

'He frightened of ME!'

'Why? What's up?'

The glint in her eye made him shudder, Dickie said.

'Last night me wanta to makka the love, but *he* no wanta to makka the love. So we do the fight!'

Dickie said he warily held out the bolts and stuff, 'This fell from the back of the washing machine!'

'What is this?'

'Just get Antonio out ... please!'

'I already told you ... he won'ta come out.'

'All right then, tell me ... has he got *any nuts*?'

Dickie then said she glared at him, then she smiled, and then she started drooling, 'I don'ta really know.' Her eyebrows were up and down like mating caterpillars according to Dickie. 'That's what I try to find out' she covered. 'I notta see *down there*, for ten years!'

By the time Dickie Manse brains-in-his-pants fell in the door, I'd managed to cobble everything together, with the aid of a spanner and a couple of wire clothes hangers. 'It's okay,' I announced proudly, 'I've fixed it, for now.'

While we were clearing up, Dickie Manse brains-in-his-pants brought up the subject of Nancy Cruddle again, 'You're not *really* going to marry her, are you?'

I told him to let it drop, or we'd end up falling out. 'Me and Nancy have named the day,' I said. 'We've already booked that fancy hotel at Caledcotte Lake so, as soon as we can get a disco, we're having the biggest engagement party you've ever seen!'

'Your mother will put a stop to it any way she can.'

'Oh no, she won't. I've already warned her, if she starts trouble, she'll be thrown out, and no messing!'

Much to everyone's horror, including my mother's, I've promised myself heart and soul and other bits to Nancy Cruddle. Yes she's got a bit of a sordid reputation, but that was all in the past.

After bumping into her at the cinema, we got talking and one thing led to another and now she wants to spend the rest of her life with me, so I'm not listening to the killjoys. Nancy loves me, and I love her, and we're having the biggest engagement party you have ever seen.

And to hell with the consequences!

BEDFORD
APRIL, TUESDAY

PAUSING FOR BREATH

These past weeks, since Nancy and I set the date for our engagement party, everything seems to be running smoothly; except for the fact that my mother has taken a real dislike to Nancy Cruddle. 'Give her a chance why don't you?' I pleaded. 'Who knows? She might well become your best friend!'

'Never!' she retorted. 'That girl is a tart, and I do not want you, or this fine family linked with a tart!'

Father argued handsomely, 'If Nancy Cruddle is what our son wants, then we have no right to interfere.'

'*You* may have no rights, but I'm his mother and it's my duty to interfere!' The smile she gave me would have turned milk sour. 'I am not happy about this engagement party.'

'So, does that mean you'll definitely refuse the invite?' I asked hopefully.

'Don't be a silly boy! You're my only son. Besides, whatever would people think if I refused to come along and support you in your hour of need?'

'What hour of need is that then?' My mother never gives up.

'Well … this thing with this … female,' her lip curled with contempt. 'We all know it's bound to go horribly wrong! And when it does, I intend to publicly accept your apology with graciousness.'

Father told her not to put such a downer on my future. 'He's old enough and ugly enough to make his own mistakes! He's made more than enough in the past without your help,' he reminded her, 'so, I'm sure he's capable of doing it again.'

'Oh, thanks a bunch, Dad!' I thought I might at least have him on my side.

'I didn't say this Nancy Crulled … thingamajig … whatever her name … was a big mistake. I'm trying to get your mother off your back, that's all…'

'Oh, is that so!' Mother was out of her chair and at his throat. 'I might have known you'd be on his side. Our son is useless … can't make the right decision to save his life! And we all know why, don't we, eh? He takes after *you*, that's why!'

Feeling like a failure, I could have given them both a piece of my mind, but I knew my dad was trying to please us both, being that he was the one caught in the middle, so I decided to make myself scarce. Besides, I'm already covered in battle scars where I've spent a lifetime coming between these two.

Once I had left, I turned my mind to more urgent matters. These next few days would be non stop! I've a party to oversee; balloons and party poppers to take along to the hotel. I needed to make sure they'd given me a big enough room and a dance floor large enough to take a crowd. Then there's the band to call, music and lighting to check out. Not to mention party bills to be settled, a new shirt and jeans to buy, flowers for my darling, and the biggest, most dazzling engagement ring that money can buy … I'm already having nightmares about the size of the loan I've taken out.

My Nancy is worth it though. These past weeks she's made my life worth living. And I don't care a toss what anyone said. They're all wrong. Nancy is a real tonic. She's warm and giving … she even shared her giant pizza with me. What other girl would do that, eh?

Oh, and she's great at sex … You would not believe the positions we get in! (I never knew I had dimples on the cheeks of my arse until she told me!) One night we were at it till the bed collapsed … then we had to pay a carpenter to repair the floorboards where the bed leg went through. Am I having fun or what?

The truth is, Nancy Cruddle is the best! She knows exactly how to treat a guy. (Dickie Manse brains-in-his-pants says it's because she's had plenty of practice … but he's only jealous, like the rest of them.)

I'm amazed at Poppy though. She's been sulking ever since she found out my intentions to Nancy are honourable.

Twice she forgot to feed the Persian cats, and the dogs were ill when she accidentally fed them with budgie droppings. It took me an hour to clean up where they sicked up all over my shoes.

One morning I found her day dreaming while the hosepipe ran over the trough and flooded the geranium patch.

'She's not good enough for you,' Poppy came into the office one day all sad and broken. 'Please listen to me, Ben. She'll break your heart.' (I didn't listen. They can all say what they like. *I* know the real Nancy, and they don't!)

Amazingly, me and Dickie Manse brains-in-his-pants, have been getting on okay; he even made me a coffee this morning (though the kettle had given up the ghost by the time I got to it…) 'It weren't me!' he said. 'I didn't break it!'

'Well who was it then?' I asked. 'If it weren't you, and it weren't me, and we're the only two in the flat, who else could it have been?'

'It was the plumber.'

'*What* plumber?'

'The one who fixed the washing machine after you cocked it up.'

'Oh, give over! That was weeks ago, and he didn't go anywhere near the kettle. Besides, it's been working all right, so how can he be to blame?'

'He let it boil for ages with the lid off.'

'So?'

'So … it's a known fact that if you leave the kettle boiling with the lid off for too long, it burns itself out.'

'Who told you that?'

'Can't remember.'

I fished in my pocket and found a twenty. 'Here!' I thrust it into his sweaty palm. 'See if you can get one next time you're near the hardware shop.'

'Can I borrow this, and get the kettle another time?' He turned his trouser pockets inside out. 'Only I'm a bit skint at the minute.'

'No!'

'Only till Friday, I promise.'

'I said NO!' I was absolutely adamant. 'Besides, you never even paid me back that tenner I lent you.'

'So, I'll give you *thirty* on Friday.'

'NO!'

'You know you said my socks were walking by themselves?'

'Don't remind me!' I still had the smell of them in my nostrils. It's true, his socks have taken on a life of their own, but Dickie and his socks are not *my* responsibility. 'READ MY LIPS! YOU ARE NOT BUYING SOCKS WITH MY MONEY!'

'Don't you want to know why I need the socks?'

'Surprise me!'

'It's your party soon, so I thought I should get a new pair … or three. And you remember Saturday, don't you … what you said about the socks walking themselves to the shower?'

'Could I ever forget?' I swear it wasn't a nightmare; I actually saw his socks, all stiff and stinky, march across the room and climb into the shower all by themselves.

'So, can I borrow the twenty till Friday?'

'You'd best not be using that money to back the horses!'

'I'm not!'

'I want to see at least four pairs of brand new socks and the receipt … before tonight!'

His smile made me nervous. 'You're a pal!' When he says that I always feel like I've been done over by a conman.

Later, I walked down the street with a smile on my face. This time on Sunday, me and Nancy Cruddle will be engaged to be married! How cool is that?

I thought about what my mother had said… 'We all know it's bound to go horribly wrong.'

'No, Mother dear!' I protested loudly (getting a few odd looks from passers by). 'It will NOT go wrong. In fact, it'll be the best party in the world, you'll see!'

In fact, it seemed at last that all was right in my world. And I wasn't about to let anyone tell me otherwise! Not Poppy, not Dickie Manse brains-in-his-pants. And certainly not my psycho mother!

Roll on Saturday, that's what I say.

Me and Nancy will make them all eat their words.

BEDFORD
APRIL, MONDAY

Dear diary, I am broken hearted!

I'm also deeply ashamed and positively suicidal. I know everybody's laughing at me behind my back, and why not, eh? I deserve it.

The truth is, not only am I the talk of the town, I'm broke, badly behind with my rent, and when I ran out of petrol the other day, I had to borrow a tenner from the ever loyal Poppy. How low is that?

Dickie Manse brains-in-his-pants offered to bail me out, and I had no choice but to accept! The trouble is, now that I'm beholden to him will he ever let me forget it?

To tell you the truth, my faith in human nature is well and truly shattered. I will never trust a woman again. I've already made a vow of celibacy, and I thoroughly intend living my life on my own (except for Dickie Manse brains-in-his-pants, who at the moment is keeping the roof over my head).

What is it with me and women, eh? Why am I such a loser? I've learned my lesson this time though. Flying in the face of my mother's advice, I made a huge mistake with Laura, the possessive, vindictive bunny-boiler I married. Then there were a few unforgettable skirmishes with the shadier members of the opposite sex, and now the insatiable Nancy Cruddle. Will I never learn?

I can't say I wasn't warned; even the woman in the paper shop tried to put me off her... 'That flighty trollop has had the pants off you, and now she's after blood.' She wagged a knowing finger. 'Tarts like that ... we women can suss 'em out a mile away, while all you men can see are the come-on eyes and long legs.'

She was right, because it was Nancy's long legs that caught my attention in the first place.

'Women like her are bad news!' she went on, still wagging her finger. 'Predators, that's what they are!'

'I'll thank you to mind your own business!' I was really fed up now. 'If you want predators, you've only got to look at your fat, lazy lump of a husband!'

I was almost out the door when the Coke can got me in the back of the neck. 'You cheeky young bugger! I'll admit my Len might be lazy, but he ain't been riding the local bike ... not like you!'

You won't be surprised to know that I was off work for three days with whiplash. It didn't matter though, because thanks to Nancy Cruddle, it suited me to hide away and sulk.

As you might have guessed, my engagement party was the party from hell! Nancy Cruddle is the only woman to have ever taken me for an idiot ... big time! (Not counting that shapely little blonde who worked the till at Tesco. She never warned me about the big, hairy husband who caught us snogging in the car park. She went off with him cool as you like, while I was left lying face down on the pavement, my jaw throbbing and my pride dented.)

The truth is I can't seem to find a sweet, innocent girl who would make my life worthwhile. Okay, I know I'm not the best catch in the world, but I'm hard working and passable, so why can't I find the girl of my dreams? I seem to attract nothing but disaster.

I mean, there's the mother from hell, and that walking catastrophe, Dickie Manse brains-in-his-pants (though he's not all that bad when you get to know him). There's my vicious ex-wife, Laura, who once threatened to cut my balls off if she ever caught me with another woman. When she saw me talking with a good-looking neighbour who was simply asking directions to the bus stop, I hardly dared go to bed that night. I mean, after what she threatened, I could have woken up without a spare part to call my own.

And y'know what? I'm sure I caught sight of the dreaded Laura, lurking suspiciously outside the hotel where the party was held.

Now I come to think of it, I wouldn't be at all surprised

if she hadn't engineered the whole horrible, humiliating episode!

It's hard to believe I did not see it coming, when everyone else did. If they knew all along, why did they come to the party? Why were the cheeky buggers eating my food and drinking my booze?

I expect they were just waiting for the show to begin. Well, they were not disappointed, because when it did kick off, it was the carnival event of the year, with me as the clown.

I really thought me and Nancy had the world at our feet. We made a big thing of announcing our engagement, then when I presented her with the white-gold diamond ring, everyone clapped (except for the lovely Poppy, who ran off, and my drunken psycho mother, who lurched between my father and the flower display, her face a picture of pure evil).

As for Dickie Manse brains-in-his-pants, he thought nobody could see him when he slunk behind the curtains with this lanky, well-endowed redhead, blissfully unaware that, thanks to the garden light behind, we could all see them as they snogged and fooled about.

When the snogging got serious, the entire room went deathly quiet; all we could hear was grunting and squealing and smacking of lips. (Everyone assumed that's what it was, but knowing Dickie Manse brains-in-his-pants, there was always room for doubt.)

You'd have thought he might have realised he was not

alone. But as we all know, he lives on another planet.

Everyone was having a good time though. Towards the end of the evening, they were all out there on the dance floor, enjoying the good music and dancing the night away (all except Dickie and his redhead, who were back behind the curtains, doing some dancing of their own). I can't understand how they didn't realise that we could see their every move; or maybe he *did* know and wanted us all to share in the fun!

We all sensed the inevitable, and we were right. It was only a matter of time before they fell through the open windows and crashed into the garden. (The elderly couple on the patio did not enjoy the experience, when they were sent careering into the swimming pool!)

'Whatever did you see in her?' I asked him later. 'Your buxom redhead looked like a bloke in drag.'

'Now you know why we fell through the window,' he muttered semi-incoherently, 'I found something I shouldn't have.'

'*What?*' The mind boggled. 'You don't mean…?'

He gave an almighty groan and collapsed at my feet. It took four of us to lay him out on a garden bench.

I've decided never again to mention the redhead. Some things are best left alone, if you ask me!

Leaving him snoring contentedly on the bench, I went in search of Nancy.

It was a cracking party. The band was first class and

when I found Nancy, I dragged her on to the crowded dance floor, ready to boogie the night away.

Everyone was merry, there was a lot of laughter and singing and drunken revelling. The band was wild, and the guitarist was out of this world! In fact some of the more reckless girls were literally throwing themselves at him; but he just carried on playing, all proud and glorious ... like a captain going down with his ship.

As for me, I couldn't take my eyes off that massive crop of wild yellow hair wrapped round his head ... bobbing up and down, thrown every which way, it couldn't have been a wig or it would have come off long since. What puzzled me was how could he see with a Labrador flopping all over his face?

'Ben?' Nancy yelled over the noise.

'What?' I leaned in closer.

'I really love this party!' She shouted again.

I was dead chuffed. 'Do you?'

'I just said so, didn't I?' I could see Nancy was a bit distracted.

'The wedding party will be even better!'

'WHAT DID YOU SAY?'

'I said ... THE WEDDING PARTY WILL BE EVEN BETTER!'

'Listen, Ben!'

'What?'

'I've got to go!'

'Aw, Nancy! We've only just got on the dance floor.' And I was having fun, arms in the air, doing the YMCA!

'LOOK!' She pointed across the room. 'It's my old school friends! There's Joanne and Elaine and … Ooh! Look … it's Lennie … I owe him a big thank you for saving me from the school bully.'

'What?'

'THE SCHOOL BULLY! He was trying to take advantage when Lennie clobbered him … Ooo, they've seen me! I must go and say hello … it's been such a long time.'

'Nancy?'

'WHAT NOW?'

'*I* can't see them.' All I could see was a forest of dancers.

'They're over there … look!'

'WHERE?'

'Don't worry. I'll introduce you later.'

'ALL RIGHT, SWEETHEART! I'LL WAIT TILL THEY'VE FINISHED YMCA AND I'LL COME AND FIND YOU!'

'No, it's all right! I'll be back in a minute.'

'BUT I WANT TO MEET YOUR OLD … SCHOOL…' I only looked away for a second and she was gone. The music stopped for an instant while the band shifted about, and then they were playing YMCA for a second time.

The trouble is, once I was in full swing, I didn't want to stop. 'DON'T WORRY, NANCY!' I yelled. 'I'LL FIND YOU AFTER!'

She was soon swallowed up in the heaving crowd. Then

the band went for a break leaving only the keyboard player. The crowd chanted for YMCA again. So there I was, having the time of my life, doing my stuff and singing along with everyone else, YMCA … du … du … du … YMCA. How brill is that? I kid you not. There is nothing to touch it.

Exhausted but delirious, I cheered like the rest of them when YMCA crashed to a finish and the keyboard player went off to enjoy a well deserved break.

'Have you seen Nancy?' I must have asked about twenty people and they all said they'd seen her a while back, but not lately.

I spent a full half hour searching inside and out, but she seemed to have vanished from the face of the earth. I even fought my way through the shrubbery – that's where I thought I saw the dreaded Laura lurking about. But I'd had a few bevvies by then, so it could have been anybody.

The bartender was useless. 'She was here for a while,' he said, 'then she asked me to tell you that if you came looking, I was to let you know she'd gone outside for some fresh air.'

So I went outside, scouring the area and fighting my way ever deeper into the shrubbery; but still no Nancy.

Half an hour later, smothered in bracken and twigs, with both arms scratched and bleeding, I staggered out looking like a tramp.

'Good grief!' The caterer was shocked. 'You poor thing.

Look, the staff are using the bathroom upstairs ... third on the right. You'd best get off and clean yourself up, before you frighten the punters.'

I never got to the bathroom.

I climbed to the top of the stairs, startling two girls as they came skipping down. 'You're not the enemy are you?' they giggled nervously, 'Parachuted in to kidnap us?'

Undaunted, I looked round for the bathroom. I had my hand on the doorknob when I heard a familiar voice coming from the room next door. Gingerly, I crept up to the door and listened; was it Nancy or not? Only one way to find out.

I put my ear to the bedroom door, and sure enough it sounded very like my Nancy. She was talking to some-body, then she was singing and then there were muffled voices mingling with the music. 'Nancy, is that you in there?' I tapped on the door, but the music was so loud inside I didn't know if she could hear me.

Suddenly there was a dirty, girly laugh, and yes! That was definitely my Nancy!

When I gingerly opened the door, I got the shock of my life! There they were, rolling round the floor as arse-bare as the day they were born. I recognised the guitarist by the Harley Davidson tattoo on his upper arm. His bald head threw me at first, until I saw the dead Labrador hanging on the bed head (it *was* a wig!).

I stood there in total shock for at least a full minute before Nancy saw me and gave a loud scream, and she kept on screaming. 'HELP! IT'S THE THING FROM THRILLER!' Stupid cow!

Wide-eyed and terrified, the guitarist reached for his clothes and his Labrador wig. In his haste he threw the Labrador on back to front and couldn't see a damned thing. 'I've caught you at it!' I was gutted. 'What have you got to say for yourself?'

'Don't shoot!' Nancy hadn't recognised me. 'Please … don't shoot!'

'My mother was right all along,' I intended to keep my dignity at all costs.

She suddenly recognised me beneath all the shrubbery, and she put on her little-girl act. 'Oh, Ben … oh, sweetheart! It's *you*! I didn't recognise … oh, and this isn't what you might think. You see … I was just helping him find his wig, that's all.' We both glanced at the guitarist, who by now was locked in a deadly struggle with his tatty hair piece.

'Oh, I see…' My lazy grin gave nothing away. 'Looking for his *wig*, were you? And with no clothes on. Well I never! That's the first time I've heard it called that!'

I did not yell. I did not resort to gutter tactics. Instead, I stayed outwardly calm but raging beneath (also twitching a bit where the nettles had somehow punctured my trousers and stung my nether-regions). 'I tell you what, Nancy … why don't you just carry on with your little game. And when you've finished "looking for his wig" you can get out of my life, because you and me are history. D'you understand what I'm saying? It's over ... for good!'

I was totally in control; no screaming, pleading or temper tantrums, and no smacking the guitarist. (I could hear him, but I couldn't see him. He'd fallen over trying to get his right limb in his left trouser-leg. I reckon he was terrified of me.)

I might have kept my control if she hadn't hobbled towards me on her knees and started clawing at my leg, 'Please, Ben ... don't take it bad. I love you and I want to marry you, I really do.'

It wasn't the fact that she was lying through her teeth that did it. Nor was it that pitiful look she gave me, with racking sobs and eyes filled with tears. No! It was because she was gripping the leg that was caked in rose thorns, which she was now accidentally driving into my flesh.

'GET AWAY FROM ME, YOU WITCH FROM HELL!' Screaming with pain I pushed her away; that was when she fell against the guitarist, and they were both on the floor in a tangle of clothes and wig. I didn't feel any sympathy though. Serves them bloody right that's what I say!

In utter agony but feeling proud of myself, I hobbled down the stairs leaving them both shouting and struggling.

Treating them with the contempt they deserved, I made my way across the hall and through the crowds that were gathering. 'It's all right,' I said, 'everything's under control. Start the music and enjoy what's left of the evening.' I had absolutely no idea why they stared back at me as though I'd recently escaped from an asylum!

I was about to go into the loo and clean myself up when the hired security men grabbed me. 'This is a private party,' they man-handled me to the front door. 'We don't want no trouble here!' They then slung me out on my face and slammed the door shut. 'AND DON'T COME BACK!'

As I lay there, bruised and battered, and plastered in jungle stuff, a small hand reached out to help me up. 'I've got the Land Rover,' she said, 'I'll take you home.'

So off we went down the path together, me and Poppy; my loyal little friend.

As for Nancy Cruddle, if I never clapped eyes on her again, it would be too soon!

Mind you, I mean to get that diamond ring back.

I desperately need it if I'm to catch up on the rent.

Judging by the excitement going on behind the see-through curtains, Dickie Manse may never surface again.

Naw! After what happened tonight, I could never be that lucky.

BEDFORD
JUNE, WEDNESDAY

Well, hello diary, here we are again, and I'm feeling really unsettled.

It's been a bit too quiet of late; although having said that, we have had the odd crazy antic from you know who!

Do you remember that tall redhead he got tied up with at my engagement party – the party that turned out to be a disaster on a mega scale?

How could you forget the pair of them going at it until they crashed through the window, sending two poor old buggers careering into the swimming pool?

Two days later, our Dickie started itching, *down there* … if you know what I mean?

It got to the point when I just could not stand it any longer. 'What the devil's wrong with you?' He was itching while he was eating his Cornflakes; then he was having a crafty scratch on his way out the door, and going down the street he was rubbing his legs together and doing the twist like you've never seen. Honest to God! One minute he was hopping and jumping along, and the next minute he was up against the corner of the wall, rubbing his back and making noises like an orang-utan in season.

It was worse at night after he'd gone to bed. The old iron bed he found in a bargain-basement shop has a habit of rocking and rolling every time he turns over, and now it was even worse.

It nearly drove me over the edge! The knob on his bed head is really loose, so when he started with the jumping and scratching, the knob rattled out a ghostly tune against my wall. It was like the march of the skelebobs all over again!

'BEN!' It was three a.m. when he came hammering on my door, 'Ben, wake up! I can't get to sleep!'

'No, and neither can I, so bugger off!' What did I have to do to get some peace?

'I've got the itch!' He wailed.

'Get back to bed and let a bloke get some sleep!' I was *not* going to get up.

Dickie moaned, 'But I need help!'

'You're not the only one!'

'BEN!'

'WHAT?'

Silence.

'DICKIE, IT'S THREE IN THE MORNING. WHAT DO YOU WANT?'

'I think I've caught the pox.'

'Who from?'

'You know!'

'How do I know?'

'Because you warned me about it.'

'Right, that's it!' I leaped out of bed (well, kinda rolled out). 'As soon as it's light I want you ready to go.'

'Go where?'

'The clinic! Where you should have gone days ago.'

'No way! You can forget that! I'm not having anyone looking and feeling my private parts…'

'That's never bothered you before.'

'Well, this time it's different!'

'How?'

Slight pause, then, 'Well, the first way is when they're looking for what makes you giggle. And the other way is when they're looking for what makes you itch.'

'Okay, but if you don't let them find out what's making you itch, I'll put the word out and you will never giggle again!'

'You wouldn't!'

'I would!'

'Okay then, I'll go, but if there's any monkey business I'm outta there!'

*   *   *

We were first in line when the clinic opened. Dickie insisted I came with him, for moral support, though I did think that was taking our friendship too far!

As it turned out, the nurse had seen it all before. 'Entering the unknown without an overcoat ... a man of your age should know better!'

'But it was high summer. Who needs an overcoat?'

'Yes? Well, who needs what you've got?' She was a real-life Hannibal Lector and I did not like the way she stared at his red red puddings!

'I haven't come here for a lecture. I've come here to cure my itch!'

'Don't you get sarky with me, young man! If anybody should be sarky, it's me. I should be settling down with my morning cuppa, and here I am, feeling some twerp's spotty nether regions.'

'My nether regions are NOT spotty!'

'Oh, I see! Telling me my job now are you? I'll have you know, you've got the makings of a serious case of gonorrhoea.'

'You're not supposed to talk to me like that.' He was well insulted, 'You're a nurse, and I'm a patient, and I will not have you rubbishing me, like I was some kind of idiot who never wears an "overcoat".'

'Well, if the cap fits...'

As Dickie turned away, she saw the rash on the back of his neck. 'What's this?' She grabbed him by the arm.

'Get off me!'

'Show me your back.'

'No!'

'Right then.' Before you could say 'taters' she had him in an arm lock. Dickie screamed for me to help, but I had no intention of going three rounds with her.

'You got yourself into this mess, get yourself out!' I was hiding behind the door.

After a fight and a tussle she called the doctor, who made a short examination and the verdict was in.

'Have you considered cosmetic surgery?' He asked.

Dickie gave him one of his glares, 'How dare you! I ought to sue the pants off you!'

'You can sue me all you like,' the doctor told him. ' I'm just saying we have some good stretching facilities here.'

He felt and pushed and shook and pulled, until Dickie was yelping in pain. 'Right! Stop that screaming and get dressed!' He was a real manly sort.

It turns out that Dickie did not have the dreaded lurgy at all. After a few questions, it emerged that the itching had been caused because Dickie Manse brains-in-his-pants had washed his underwear in the stuff I got to flush out the drains.

'You've wasted our time!' The doctor was not happy, 'So is there anything else you'd like me to examine?'

'No thanks!' Dickie ran out the door like his ass was on fire.

The doctor looked at me, 'On the couch please – I'll take a look at you now.'

I overtook Dickie down the corridor.

The following morning, Antonio from the chippie called us in. 'My wife said I havva to speaka with you both.' He looked dead serious.

Poor Dickie was still sore from lack of sleep, on account of the fact that he'd been awake half the night, scrubbing his nether regions with soap, after being man-handled by the nurse. 'Leave us alone … I'm not well,' he groaned.

'I donta care!' He really meant trouble. 'You listen to me!' he snarled. 'My wife says I musta find out.'

'Find out what?' I was curious.

'You anda thisa one,' he pointed to Dickie Manse brains-in-his-pants, '…didda you havva the women last night?' His bushy eyebrows went up.

'Huh!' Dickie Manse was in a mood. 'Chance would be a fine thing, only my tackle isn't working properly.'

I told him straight. 'We did *not* havva the women last night.'

'So why havva you beena banging all the night?'

'Oh, that was just the knob against the wall, but you see…' I paused discreetly, to lower my voice. 'It was Dickie's fault.' I gave him what I thought was a knowing look. 'You see … he had a little itch.'

'Haha!' Winking at me, Antonio then rolled his eyes at

134

Dickie. 'You lucky man to havva the woman, eh?' His eye-brows were going up and down like two hairy worms. 'Dickie getta the itch, and the woman make itta better, eh?'

When Dickie was about to launch into a full explanation, I drew him away. 'Let Antonio have his little delusions,' I said. 'He doesn't get much else.'

In fact it made Antonio's day. As we went away, he was smiling and winking and giving Dickie a knowing smile. Then his wife came out, clipped him round the ear and dragged him off. 'Maybe you havva the itch too, eh?' She was smiling from ear to ear. 'Mamma fix it for you, yes?' She winked at Dickie, and slammed shut the door.

Wow! It might be Antonio's lucky day after all.

BEDFORD
JUNE, SATURDAY

Hello, diary. You won't believe what Dickie's been up to now. It all started on Saturday morning.

'LET ME IN!' I thought Dickie was about to knock the door down. 'BEN! OPEN THE DOOR. I'VE GOT MY HANDS FULL!'

I opened the door and this enormous, yellow daisy fell on top of me, almost crushing me under its weight. Made of wood and with a bulbous red eye, it was the most awful monstrosity. 'Where the devil did you get this?'

'From a car boot sale … two quid it cost me, and worth every penny!'

'Two quid! They must have seen you coming! It looks like a leftover from *The Day of the Triffids*!' The big red eye was staring right at me. 'Get it out! I do not want that thing in this flat!'

'NO!' Dickie struggled through the door with it. 'This is

my flat as well. You can't stop me having what I like in my half.'

As if the daisy wasn't enough, he started dragging another monstrosity in through the door. 'Don't tell me there's more!'

'Ah, but you'll like this,' he said proudly, '…this is a talking point. It's entertaining … and…'

'What is it?'

He ripped off the paper, 'TA DAA!' There was a huge, bulbous thing, which looked like a mirror, but not like a mirror, if you get my drift. 'What's that supposed to be?'

'It's a trick thing!' Standing it up against the wall, he backed away, 'Go and have a look.'

I looked and saw what was supposed to be me, only my nose was floating on my knee; one of my eyes juggled on my forehead and the other winked at me from my shoulder. 'Bloody Nora!' I threw the wrapping paper over it. 'You've got to be joking if you think that thing is coming to live in this flat.'

'Don't be such a big girl's blouse! Just think of the fun we'll have. We could hang it in the loo, and when our mates come round they'll go for a leak and see this *huge misshapen* monster staring back at them.' He chuckled, 'No, idiot, I didn't mean… *that* … "monster". I meant the mirror … when they see themselves in it…'

'I know what you meant and the answer is no!' All the shouting woke up Battersby. Wide-eyed and startled he galloped across the room and caught a glimpse in the mirror. When he saw what looked like the Yeti staring back at him, he went crazy, throwing himself at the mirror, then yapping and running about in circles, eyes wild and teeth showing. The more he yapped at it the more the image yapped back.

'Get him out of here!' The noise was doing my head in. 'Antonio will be up here next, giving us notice to quit!'

'Get down!' Dickie grabbed the dog by the collar. 'It's not another dog, you four-legged twerp ... it's *you* ... only a bit bigger...' By now, the dog was going into a frenzy.

The thing in the mirror was moving all about and twisted beyond recognition. Its head was on its rear end and its tail was waving like a feather from the back of its neck. The eyes were all over the place, and when I laughingly told the dog to 'KILL!' it launched itself into the air straight into the mirror, which exploded into a million fragments, half of which went crashing down the stairs and shuddered to a halt.

When Battersby chased after it, he saw thousands of eyes staring at him from every angle and tails wagging like snakes about to strike. It was all too much. With his tail between his legs, he sped out the door squealing and howling like a banshee. In his panic the dog careered into the postman, who ended up in the gutter with the mail blowing in the wind.

It wouldn't surprise me if we never saw him again, the

dog I mean; or even the postman, judging by the way he legged it down the street.

'Watsa going on 'ere?' Antonio's wife ran into the hallway, saw herself in the fragments of mirror and yelled for Antonio, 'HUSBANDA! LOOK WHAT THEY'VE'A DONE TO ME!'

'Husbanda' came skidding in, saw his wife in the mirror and collapsed in hysterics, 'LOOK ATTA YOU!' Grabbing her by the shoulders, he gave her a playful push so she shifted to a different, more frightening version of herself. 'Itsa funny, no?' he laughed.

'You 'orrible husbanda!' She clapped him on the ear and sent him careering to the door. 'YOU CRAZY NO-GOOD!' Waving her arms about, she caught sight of herself in the mirror; floating bits of face leered back at her, her nose ten times its size, all twisted and grotesque; when she yelled her mouth was a big, black cavern that could have swallowed us whole. 'IF YOU DONTA GET THIS THING OUTTA MY PLACE, I WILL KILL YOU ALL!' Gawd! We must have really touched a nerve.

Still ranting, Maria got Antonio by the scruff of his collar and dragged him off.

'I can't believe you've done it again!' I rounded on Dickie Manse brains-in-his-pants. 'You cause more trouble than you're worth. You know what … I've a good mind to leave you and find a place of my own. That way I might just keep my sanity.'

'You wouldn't do that, would you?' Dickie had this sorry, gormless look on his face.

'Oh yes, I would!' In the pieces of broken mirror I caught sight of me and him on the floor; teeth talking to the ears and arms growing from the side of my head. I couldn't help but laugh. 'You're a walking disaster!' I moaned.

'You'd be bored out of your mind if I wasn't around though. Go on, admit it.'

He was right.

It took a while to clear up the mess, because we were laughing too much.

What really set us off was Antonio and his wife yelling at each other. 'Whatta we gonna do about them two?' Antonio wailed.

'Shutuppa the mouth,' Maria told him. 'We'll get rid of them ... specially Tricky Dickie man. He frightening me too much!'

Roll on Monday when I'm back at the kennels. It's a doddle compared to life at home with him!

BEDFORD
JULY, THURSDAY

Well, here I am again, diary, worn out, fed up, tired and badly in need of a holiday.

We had six kittens born a few weeks ago, from a stray cat somebody found cowering in their shed. No sooner was the poor thing settled with us, she promptly gave birth. Thankfully, we've already managed to find homes for each and every kitten.

Andy the new boy got drenched again; that's the third time since he started here, and it's all thanks to Poppy. She's a loose cannon at times; a light gone out! (But we all love her, really.)

She thought she'd switched the hosepipe off at the nozzle, then she went back to turn on the tap; but of course the nozzle was active and right in line for the first hosing was the new boy. 'HELP!' The poor thing, he's always yelling for help, 'TURN IT OFF!'

While he was busy screaming, a bulky shadow leaped up from the hedge and took flight. Was it a bird? No! Was it a cloud? No! It was my dreaded ex, Laura, dripping wet and fleeing for her life without so much as a how d'you do.

'Serves you right, you mad stalker!' I shouted as she slunk off, 'At least the water can't shrink your brain any more, eh?' When she clapped her hands to her ears, I thought she was trying to shut me out, until I remembered she always did that when she'd had a new hairdo; if it was raining, or the wind was blowing, and she didn't have a hat or hood, she would flatten her hands to her head to keep her hair from spiralling out of control. Silly bat!

'I hope your wig falls off!' I let her know I was none too pleased about her skulking in my bushes!

Meanwhile, Poppy ran back to turn off the hose, slipped in the puddle and took off like a snowboard down a mountain, slithering all the way, laughing and shouting, and generally enjoying herself.

When she ended up in the open kennel I told Andy to lock her in, and the silly bugger took me at my word. Then the locks seized up and we couldn't get her out.

To make matters worse, some bloke arrived with a delivery. 'Can I buy that little beauty in there?' He pointed to Poppy.

'No, you bloody well can't,' she yelled, and threw a dog biscuit at him. It caught him in the eye and temporarily blinded him.

I was three hours at the hospital, waiting for them to check him out. When he emerged he was wearing an eye patch, 'I'll have you for this!' he threatened.

I told him, 'Have me all you like, you won't be the first.' He can make of that what he will. I'm past caring!

BEDFORD
AUGUST, SATURDAY

Well, diary, the excitement never ends!

Me and Dickie Manse have decided to meet up after work. Having upset him once again, we promised Antonio that we'd paint his back yard, and we would provide the paint. So off we went to the B&Q store again. We were hoping they wouldn't recognise us from the last time we were there.

'Ooh, look! There's a sale on!' Dickie always gets excited when there's a sale on. It doesn't matter what they're selling, if it's two for one, he'll buy three.

At least the sale had improved his mood. 'I don't see why we have to paint his yard anyway!' He'd moaned all the way there, 'It's not as if they're paying us for doing the job.

'No, but if you can remember not to antagonise them, we'll have a roof over our heads, which we could easily have lost, thanks to you!'

'What d'you mean? It wasn't my fault that tap flew off the bathroom wall and the water came through their ceiling.'

'So who else's fault was it then?'

'I don't know. All I know is, it wasn't me!'

When his eager eyes alighted on the paint department, he went off at a trot, 'What colour did he say he wanted?'

'Antonio didn't say. He said he was happy to leave it to us. As long as it wasn't black, red or purple, he didn't mind.'

The shelves were filled with every colour of paint imaginable, 'There's a nice pale green in the sale corner,' Dickie said. 'Ooh, look at that! Half price an' all!' (As I said, it takes very little to get him excited.)

'Right!' I followed him to the sale corner. 'For once, Dickie my friend, you are spot on. That's a good choice. Pale green, he can't argue with that, cos it'll match the mould growing up the walls.'

We bought four large cans, and then went for a quick pint to celebrate.

When we got back to the chip shop, Antonio was at the door, almost as though he was waiting for us. 'Whatta colour didda you get?'

We showed him, and would you believe, he actually liked it, and so did Maria, who came running out to see what was up. 'Bellissima!' she shouted, arms in the air, 'You do something right for once, eh? BELLISSIMA!'

'No need to swear!' Dickie was offended.

'I no swear!' she protested, 'I very pleased.'

'When do you want it painted?' I asked.

'Tonightta!' Antonio went on, 'Me and that...' he jerked a thumb in the direction of his other half, 'We go outta together.' His smile was so scary, I wondered if he was planning to do away with her. 'We havva the celebrations tonightta. We beena married twenty-five years.'

'Wonderful!' I thought of me and Laura... twenty-five years, eh? Jeez! Was that a life sentence, or was that a life sentence!

While the two of them went back inside, arguing all the way, we carried the paint through to the back yard. 'Look at the height of them walls!' Dickie Manse looked terrified, 'Don't tell me we've got to paint all four walls?'

'Oh, yes,' I knew that because Antonio had been very particular, '...every brick, every nook and cranny, that's what he said.'

Dickie groaned from his boots, 'Can we go back down the pub for a bevvy and a pie first?'

'No! You heard what he said. They're off to celebrate so they'll be gone within the hour, and we can get started. We'll go down the pub afterwards. Okay?'

We changed into our painting clothes and enjoyed a sandwich and a drink. Then the minute we heard them leave, we were down there, ready to start.

It took us three hours of back-breaking work. We painted every square inch of that yard, the seven-foot walls, and even the back gate, and when we stood back to review our handiwork, I was dead chuffed, and so proud that Dickie Manse brains-in-his-pants had actually done a good job.

'You've excelled yourself,' I told him. 'We've painted everything, and you haven't even spilled one single drop of paint.'

He went all silly, 'That's the first time you've ever praised me.'

'Well, you deserve it. You worked hard. You found the sale department. You chose the colour, and now it looks an absolute treat. Well done that man!'

I swear Dickie blushed bright pink (or it could be the exertion of work).

'Do you think he'll reduce our rent?' he asked.

'Well, you never know, he might just do that, seeing as we've saved him a fortune.'

We didn't go to the pub, we were too knackered! We grabbed what was left in the fridge, finished off the last two beers, and while Dickie Manse fell asleep on the sofa, I shuffled off to my room and went out like a light.

I was in the middle of a nightmare (or I thought I was) when I woke up and there was all this screaming and shouting.

'Quick!' Dickie Manse was hammering on my door, 'GET UP! BEN, GET UP! They're back, and they're going crazy!'

Leaping out of bed, I threw my curtains back and was instantly blinded. It was like the aliens had landed. Downstairs in the yard I could see two little figures running round, like lawnmowers out of control.

Dickie fell into my room, 'LOOK AT IT!' he yelled, 'LOOK WHAT YOU'VE DONE!'

The whole back street was lit up and the yard was like a UFO. 'What is it?' I yelled, 'What's going on?'

'It's luminous!' he yelled, 'THE BLOODY PAINT IS PSYCHEDELIC!'

I peered down. The entire neighbourhood was bathed in a pale green luminous glow. There were people in the streets all looking up, arms reaching to the skies and a look of puzzlement on their faces.

'Bloody Nora!' I grabbed Dickie, 'Get in here!' I told him. 'LOCK THE DAMNED DOOR!'

We stayed locked in, huddled and terrified until the morning, when everything was back to normal, with one exception. Antonio locked in the yard, while we repainted the walls in white wash.

'You mad! Gone out of the mind! Maniac, bloody crazy idiots!' Antonio was wearing sunglasses, 'You havva no brains!'

(No energy neither, by the time we finished that lot!)

'You wanttta locking uppa!' When he got excited he started screeching in his native tongue. We didn't know whether he was congratulating us on a job well done, or whether he was threatening to do away with us. There was a moment when I thought he said, 'You ought to be dead, I bring in the mafia.'

I didn't sleep a wink that night. I had visions of the mafia bursting into my room and doing away with me.

In the morning I tackled him and found out I'd got it wrong.

What he apparently said was, 'You wrong in the head, I think you get daffier!' And you know what, he's absolutely right.

BEDFORD
SEPTEMBER, FRIDAY

It's Friday night, diary, and I'm all geared up for a weekend in Blackpool. By now the illuminations will be turned on, and according to rumour, they get better every year so, judging by the last time I saw them, I reckon they'll be spectacular.

I had planned to escape without you know who in tow, but unfortunately he brought in the post and opened what he thought was a circular. Of course it would have to be my hotel reservation wouldn't it?

'Some mate you are!' he wailed. 'I can't believe you would do that to me.' I thought he was about to burst into tears, 'Since that business with the paint and then being locked in the yard like a criminal, I've been living on the edge. I need to get away as much as you do, and here you are jetting off on your own behind my back … you're a selfish no-good article, that's what you are!'

I was not having that, so I told him straight, 'We are not tied to each other.' I laid the law down good and proper, 'I don't need you to know everything I'm planning. I don't need your permission to go away for a break, and I do not need you hanging on my shirt-tails wherever I go. So, if I fancy going somewhere without telling you, I've got every right to do so! I've taken a few days off work, and I'm away to Blackpool. On my own. By myself. Me alone – especially without you!' There! That told him.

He got all uppity. 'I don't like the tone of your voice,' he whimpered, 'and what are you implying ... hanging on to your shirt-tails indeed.'

'I'm not implying anything. I just don't want you thinking you can run my life, just because we share a flat. The fact is I've been through a lot lately...'

'Yes, and so have I!'

'Not as much as me. For a start you don't have to put up with some twit like you, who you trust to buy proper paint and who turns the entire neighbourhood into something out of a science fiction horror!'

'Maybe not, but it was me who had to do the top of the walls again; it was me who had to climb the ladder, and it was me who had to clear up afterwards.'

'Quite right too! It was you who caused the whole mess in the first place!'

'I wouldn't have, if you had chosen the paint instead of

making me do it, and now I'm a bag of nerves, and I need a holiday. Please!'

'You're a bag of nerves, are you? Well, I'm at breaking point. I've been really down since that disastrous engagement party. My ex is stalking me big time, and Poppy is driving me crazy, peering round corners at me and then running off. If I don't get away, I think I'll go out of my mind. So, I'm taking a few days off, and I'm heading for Blackpool.'

'I can have my bag packed and be ready in five minutes tops. PLEASE?'

He was trying his old tricks to make me feel guilty again, and wasn't having it. 'Dickie?'

'What?'

'Read my lips! *You are NOT coming*, and that's an end to it!'

'So, you don't want me with you, is that what you're saying?'

Gordon Bennett! Can you believe him?

'No, Dickie! I do not want you with me. Now if you don't mind, it's not up for discussion!'

Right up to midnight he threw tantrums; he sulked and moaned, and even threatened to wreck the place while I was gone. I told him, 'You do that, and you'd best not be here when I get back!'

'Take me with you then?'

'NO!' I reminded him, 'You need to be here to take care of the dog.'

'I'll bring him with me. He's no trouble.'

155

'The answer is no!'

'I'll put him in the kennels then. Or I'll get Antonio to look after him while we're away.'

'I said No!'

'I'll tell your ex where you've gone.'

'You wouldn't!'

'I would.'

'I reckon you would too. Right then, I'm not going to Blackpool. I'll just take off and go somewhere else, and nobody will know where I am.'

'What? Not even me?'

'Especially not you!'

'I'll follow you. I'll sit up all night and wait for you to leave, then I'll follow you, and I don't care if it's the other side of the world, because I'll have my passport with me. I've got money saved and the right to take two weeks off, because I haven't taken my owed leave yet.'

'Okay.'

'Okay … what?'

'Okay, I'll take you with me.' A plan was hatching even as I told him, 'First thing in the morning, you go and make it right with your boss, and I'll have a bag packed and wait for you until you get back.'

He made a very nasty face; even nastier than usual. 'You must think I'm stupid!'

'That's rubbish! I don't think you're stupid at all. Just a pain in the arse!'

'I don't have to make it right with my boss. I can just call him. Anyway, he doesn't really need me right now. He's got a student doing work experience. He told me the other day that I could take my leave whenever I wanted.

I was disappointed, but not beaten, 'All right. Call him in the morning. Pack your bag tonight, and we'll be away early. Okay?'

'Okay.' He was over the moon, 'I meant to watch a film tonight, but I'll download it off iplayer instead. I want to make sure I'm up bright and early.' He marched off to the kitchen, 'Want a beer?'

'No, best not. If I have one, I'll want two, and if I have two, I'll want another, and then I'll be fit for nothing, let alone driving to Blackpool.'

'A coffee then?'

'No. It's bound to keep me awake.'

'Can you lend me a few quid?'

'What the hell for?'

'To pay my hotel room.'

'You said you had savings!'

'I lied!'

'All right.'

'All right ... what?' His eyes popped out of his head, 'You mean ... you'll lend me some money?'

'I mean I'll pay for your room, but I want the money back with interest. Agreed?'

'That's mean!' he nagged, 'I always lend you money when you're a bit short, and I never ask for interest.'

'When have I ever asked you for money?'

'Can't remember.'

'That's because I have never asked you!' Dickie had conveniently forgotten he'd lent me rent money after the Nancy Cruddle incident, but I was not about to remind him.

'Well, you might one day. Anyway look, you pay for the hotel and the next time we go anywhere for a break, I'll pay for your room. Then you won't owe me anything and I won't owe you anything. That's fair, isn't it?'

I never could follow his reasoning, 'You live in cloud-cuckoo land you do!'

'But we're agreed. Right?'

'Right!' It was easy to agree; especially as he would not be coming with me.

I went to bed and sat up until he was fast asleep and snoring like a good 'un. Then I waited for half an hour before sneaking downstairs with my bag; the loud snoring playing a tune as I went.

EARLY SATURDAY MORNING

I crept out of the house and got into the car. I started the engine and set off, free as a bird, thrilled to have left him behind, snoring and all. It's not that I don't care for Dickie, because he's my mate. Now and again though, I need to clear my head and be by myself. That's not too much to ask.

I turned on the radio and sang along. There was no one to upset or follow me: no Laura, no Poppy, no mad women with poodles that wanted a haircut, nobody going manic with the water hose, and best of all, no Dickie Manse brains-in-his-pants!

The old car was doing all right until suddenly I could smell burning, like the engine was on fire, 'Oh no, that's all I need!' As I slowed down the smell got stronger and my heart sank to my boots, 'I'm gonna die in this car, burned to a crisp…'

'It's not the engine, you prat! It's the dog. Them chicken leftovers must have gone off. Sorry, mate!'

Looking in my rear-view mirror, I saw Dickie leering back at me. 'YOU!' Swerving out of control, and with the two of us screaming, I skidded to a halt on the grass verge, 'YOU DAMNED IDIOT!' I swung round, the dog leaped up from the floor and the stench from his rear end took my breath away. When he loudly trumped again it was the last straw. 'GET OUT!' I screeched, 'BOTH OF YOU … OUT OF MY CAR!'

In fact we all had to get out, or be poisoned.

I felt sick, and it wasn't just the smell (which in hindsight could have been the dog or Dickie I wasn't sure). The thing that really terrified me was the idea of that dog and Dickie, in Blackpool, in my hotel.

In fact, would they accept the dog?

More to the point, would they accept Dickie Manse brains-in-his-pants? Not if they'd got any sense they wouldn't!

'How come you got in the car so quickly?' I can be so naïve at times, 'I'm sure I heard you snoring as I came out.'

'I guessed what you were up to, so I made a tape,' he boasted. 'But before you start panicking, I slipped a note under Antonio's door asking him to turn the recorder off.' He gave this knowing grin, 'I should have asked him to look after Battersby, shouldn't I?'

'Yes, good idea! I could be unbelievably cruel, 'With luck he might have mashed him up and put him in the battered fish cakes.'

'Wicked swine.'

'You should have put him in the kennels,' I argued.

'Who? Antonio?'

'Don't be daft! I meant your smelly dog, and besides, Poppy has a soft spot for him.'

'She's got a soft spot for you an' all!' He said with a wink. 'I've seen the way she ogles your bum when you walk down the drive.'

'Don't be daft! Anyway, I expect Poppy already has a boyfriend!'

'Only because she can't have you!'

'Right! That's enough! Stop arguing.'

'I'm not arguing!'

160

'You are!'

'NOT!'

'ARE!'

'Shut up!'

'Who says?'

'Me!'

'Why don't *you* shut up?'

Heaven help us, Blackpool … here we come!

ON THE ROAD
SEPTEMBER, SATURDAY

Dear diary,

Thanks to Dickie Manse brains-in-his-pants, the trip to Blackpool turned out to be my worst nightmare; the journey was an absolute fiasco.

That stinky mutt was so full of wind we had to stop every few miles and throw him out. Then, what with Dickie moaning that he was hungry enough to faint, we had to pull in at every service station along the motorway. Altogether we added two hours to the journey.

'Are you sure the hotel allows dogs?' Setting off for the umpteenth time, Dickie wailed on about the mutt, 'I'm not staying without Battersby! We'll sleep on the beach if we have to!'

'Do what you like!' I told him straight, 'As for me, I'm gonna curl up in a soft, warm bed. My days of sleeping rough are over!'

Dickie threw a sulk, 'You know what's wrong with you?'

'I expect you're about to tell me.'

'You're old before your time, that's what!'

'Huh! *You're* older than me!'

'So?'

'So you should be the sensible one.'

'I am!'

'Not!'

'Am!'

'All right then. Who insisted on coming off the motorway to find a quiet lane?'

'Me.'

'That's right!'

'Only because Battersby needed to do his business.'

'Why didn't you make him hang on?'

'I would have, only you said he stank.'

'That's putting it mildly!'

'You don't like him, do you? Don't deny it!'

'I can't understand why he didn't go at the service station.'

'There was nowhere private for him to go. No woods, no big lorries, and no dark corners to hide in.'

'Don't be daft! He's just a dog. They don't care where they do it.'

'He might be a dog, but he's shy, and he's a thinker; he has his principles. Anyway, how would you like to go in full view of everyone?'

There was a kind of lopsided logic in his argument, 'All

right, so when we found that hedge in the back lane, why didn't he just do his business and get back to the car? Why did he have to cause such chaos?'

Dickie went into a sulk. 'It wasn't his fault; he cocked his leg and ended up in a deep ditch. How was he to know what was lurking behind that hedge!'

'So, why did *you* have to throw yourself in after him?'

'I had no choice. You saw how upset he was … all that crying and shouting…'

'That was *you*, not the dog.'

'If you'd only helped me, I would never have lost my footing!'

'And *I'll* never understand how the two of you ended up at opposite ends of the ditch.'

'I already told you what happened! The rain loosened the earth and when it collapsed in great clumps, it just carried me with it.'

'Not far enough though!'

'You don't mean that … do you?'

Maybe I didn't really mean it, but I was at the end of my tether. The original idea had been to steal away on my own and get my head together after a really hard time at the kennels. I was crushed when I discovered I had squatters in my car; a whimpering, cowering dog and a slimy, mud-caked Dickie.

Then the rain came down like heaven's hardest. I lost my way and then I didn't know where I was.

'Look, Ben. Turn left … quick!' Dickie had spied a grimy little street with a sign that said: FOOD AND DRINK – HOT AND TASTY.

'Look! The arrow points down there.'

'All right! All right! I can see for myself!'

'Go on then, put your foot down!'

I put my foot down, and drove twice up and down the grim little street, but there was nothing that resembled a café.

'Somebody's messed with the sign!' I was really worried now. 'We'd best find a route back to the motorway.'

'Not yet! The sign definitely said there's a café. We must have gone past it. Try again!' Dickie was adamant.

I glanced in the rear-view mirror to see a pathetic, shivering dog and a wild-eyed, mud-spattered Dickie – the pair of them breathing down my neck. It was like the Twilight Zone, 'Get back, the pair of you.' I felt really nervous, 'Get back now, or I'm heading home!'

They backed off and I drove down the street again and there, tucked in between two derelict shops, was a grubby little café. 'THERE IT IS!' Dickie was leaping up and down, and the mutt had me by the neck so I couldn't see a thing. I was near fainting from the toxic fumes he breathed all over me, 'GET THE DAMNED THING OFF ME!'

With the mighty Battersby slobbering down my shoulders, and Dickie leaping about like crazy, I could hardly control the car, let alone see where I was going. 'PULL OVER!' Dickie yelled at me, 'PULL OVER NOW!'

Dazed, bruised and totally disorientated, I pulled over and locked all the doors. 'I'm not getting out of this car!' They could torture me all they like, but I was not going to give in. 'I'm going home!' I really did not like the look of the place.

'Why not? It looks all right to me. It's got a menu in the window and an OPEN sign hanging on the door. Besides, all the lights are on, and I can see somebody moving about in there.'

'Where?' I peered through the gloom, 'All I can see are some little tables and a counter. If you see somebody moving it's probably the resident ghost. I say we go on and find somewhere else.'

'NO!' Dickie insisted. 'All we need is a sandwich, a drink, and a place for me and Battersby to clean up.'

'Well, I vote we move on. This place makes me nervous.'

I was about to drive away when the dog leaped over the seat and straight into my lap, 'GET OFF!' I fought like a hero. 'GET HIM OFF!'

'He's turned against you.' Dickie was enjoying himself. 'Switch the engine off, or he'll have your throat out.'

Pinned to the seat by half a ton of aggressive dog, and mad-eyed Dickie peering at me in the mirror, my sense of survival kicked in. Carefully reaching between Battersby's legs, I turned off the engine. 'All right! NOW GET HIM OFF ME!'

'Battersby! Come on, boy.' The mutt leaped over the seat and into Dickie's arms, releasing a huge puff of gas as he went.

'Oh, phew!' Half poisoned, I scrambled out of the car, 'You and that mutt are an embarrassment! If I had any sense, I'd leave you here.'

'Stop moaning. Once we're clean and fed, we won't be any trouble.'

'Huh! Famous last words!' After we all got out, I quickly locked the car before they could get back in, 'Half an hour!' I warned. 'Then we need to find a route back to the motorway.'

We sauntered smartly across the pavement, well at least I did. Dickie and the mutt just shuffled and slid, covered in slime and mud as they were.

'You're right,' Dickie admitted. 'This place does look a bit run down, but we'll be in and out before you know it. I need a quick wash and brush up; I expect Battersby needs a hedge to cock his leg up, and we're all in need of refreshment. Right?'

'Right!' It didn't look like I had much choice. 'Let's get to it!'

Showing who was boss, I led the way to the café, tried the door, and when it wouldn't open I knocked very loudly on the glass panel. 'HELLO IN THERE!' I can be assertive when I'm put out, 'WE'RE THREE WEARY TRAVELLERS IN NEED OF SUSTENANCE!'

The door slowly creaked open, just enough for a shadowy face to peer out at us, "Ow many are yer, did yer say?" We thought it was female, but the voice was low and croaky; the face lost in a murk.

'There are three of us … me, my friend Dickie, and his big, hairy mutt.'

The face looked at me, then it looked at Dickie, 'Where's the big, hairy one?'

I brought her attention to Battersby, who was skulking behind Dickie, 'This is him.'

The little eyes swivelled downwards and took stock of Battersby, 'It's not too pretty is it?' The creature twitched her nose, 'Don't *smell* too pretty neither!' She lifted her gaze to Dickie, who to my mind smelled worse than the mutt, 'What's this?'

'This is Dickie, my flatmate. The dog fell down a ditch and Dickie fell in after him. I can see I don't need to tell you how badly they stink.'

'Hmm! It'll tek a few buckets o' water to get rid o' that pong!'

'Have you got a bath they could use?'

'Might have!'

'So can they use it?'

'No, it's mine! I don't allow strangers in my bath. So what else do you want?'

'Do you have food?'

'Did yer see the sign at the top of the road?'

169

'The one that said there was a café?'

'That's the one!'

'Yes, we saw it. That's why we're here. We came off the motorway and got lost. We're all famished and like I said, these two had a bit of an accident and they need to clean up.'

'What kind of accident?'

I sighed patiently. I could see I was going to have to repeat everything. 'The dog needed to pee, so we came off the motorway and found a quiet lane. There was this hedge. He cocked his leg and the next thing we knew he was drowning in the ditch. Dickie went in after him and got washed away in the mud.'

'That's why they stink then?' The lump looked them up and down again, 'They can wash in the outside loo.'

'That'll do, yes, thank you, but we're hungry and cold. So now, can we come in?'

Ever so quietly the door opened wider. Standing before us, bathed in twilight, was the biggest, ugliest creature I have ever seen. Wrapped in a filthy pinafore, her purple matted hair forced into a ribbon over her right ear, she had bright crimson lipstick gaumed all round her mouth and down to her chin. (I hoped it was lipstick and not blood.) 'Are yer coming in or what?' she grumbled in a deep, northern accent.

Somewhat nervous we groped through the haze to search out a table, 'The fire's gerring old,' she groaned, '…too much smoke.'

Walking on the tips of his great pads, the mutt brought up the rear, watching the stranger's every move, a low growl emitting from his throat.

'Does 'e bite?' she asked.

'Only if he's worried,' Dickie said.

'Is he worried now?'

'Not yet, no.' I added cautiously.

'What does 'e eat?'

'Anything that moves.' That got her thinking.

'That's what I need, a dog that'll eat owt that moves! Is it for sale?'

'NO HE'S NOT!' Dickie was horrified. 'He's mine! I've had him since he was a pup. I love him and he loves me. He'll NEVER be for sale!'

There was a moment of palpable silence while the creature stared at Dickie and he stared back, and the mutt spread his legs as if he was about to pounce. The silence thickened, the smoke billowed round us and a clock ticked loudly in the background. It was like showdown at the OK Corral.

'BATTERSBY, SIT!' On Dickie's instructions, the mutt sat back on his haunches. We sat at the table, and the creature shuffled off, only to return a moment later with a candle. 'The lights keep flickering.' She plonked the candle on to the table. 'But yer don't need much light for eating; long as yer know where yer mouth is.' An unearthly chuckle echoed around the room. Unnerved, the mutt

howled and the stranger growled in response, 'SHUT THI
GOB OR I'LL MEK YER INTO SAUSAGES!'

'Hey you!' Dickie said nervously. 'Don't go upsetting
him like that.'

For what seemed forever she gave him the evil eye,
before the spell broke. 'Right then! I ain't got all night. The
menu is up there on the blackboard. Now then, what d'you
want?' She stood at the ready with pen and pad.

'I fancy eggs or something,' Dickie was quick to decide.

'What sort of eggs?' Still scribbling on the pad, she
didn't even look up.

'Just eggs!' He quipped bravely, 'You know ... them
oval-shaped things that pop out of a chicken's rear end!'

There was another long silence before she asked, 'What
sort of eggs are yer wanting?'

'What sort have you got?'

'Look at yon board!' She pointed to the far wall, where
the menu was chalked up in a child's scrawl.

Straining his eyes to master the higgledy-piggledy writing, Dickie read out loud: 'Fried eggs, sliced eggs, poached
eggs, scrambled eggs, boiled eggs...'

'So which d'yer want then?' She was growing impatient.

'Mmm.' Dickie knew straight off what he wanted, 'I'll
have a cheese omelette.'

'A *what*?' She gave him a look.

'An omelette, please ... with cheese.'

'So yer saying yer want a cheese omelette then?'

'That's it! Cheese omelette. Lovely!'

'This cheese omelette … is it on't board?'

Dickie checked the blackboard, 'No.' He glanced up, 'Why?'

'Well, because if it's not on't board, we don't do it!'

'But it says you do eggs every which way!'

'What was it yer wanted again?'

'An omelette!' Growing impatient, and convinced she must be a bit deaf, he raised his voice, 'I WOULD LIKE AN EGG OMELETTE … WITH CHEESE!'

'I'm not deaf!'

'Could have fooled me!' Dickie muttered under his breath.

'D'yer want trouble?'

'No, I do not want trouble!'

'And are yer saying it's not there, on't board?'

'Yes, that's exactly what I'm saying.'

'There yer are then!' Leaning forward she glared at him, 'Like I already told yer … if it's not on't board, we don't do it!'

'That's plain daft! By the look of that menu, you've got more eggs than you know what to do with, so what's so difficult about making me an egg omelette?'

She leaned towards him again, her voice low and threatening, 'D'ye see that door?'

Dickie nodded, 'Yes, so what?'

'If yer don't like what we're offering, there's the way out!' With mouth pursed and arms folded, she was a frightening sight. 'There's no chance of an omelette! Ave you got that?'

Mumbling under his breath, Dickie nodded, 'Got it, yes!'

'So I tek it you'll be leaving then?'

Before he could answer, she lunged forward, grabbed him by the ear and frog-marched him to the door. Dickie was screaming like a baby and Battersby was trotting behind, tail between his legs. I made a hasty exit too!

'Well done, that's all we needed!' As she slammed the door shut, I turned on Dickie Manse brains-in-his-pants, 'Why couldn't you have gone for poached eggs, or scrambled eggs, or other eggy things on the board?'

'Cos I fancied an omelette!' he couldn't help himself. 'That thing in there, she wants locking up! Did you see how she grabbed me by the ear?' He fondled his glowing earlobe, 'It's cabbage red, isn't it? And don't lie, cos I can feel it, all swollen and throbbing!'

There we were, without food or drink, and Dickie and Battersby still caked in foul-smelling mud. 'You're a disgrace!' I told him straight. 'You shouldn't even be here. This was my break, away from you and that disgusting hound.' I scrambled into the car and before I could start the engine, they were in the back, Battersby still whining, and Dickie still grumbling.

'It's a café, isn't it? They do eggy things, don't they? So what's wrong with wanting an omelette? Why wasn't it on the bloody board anyway! What's the difference between scrambled eggs and an omelette, tell me that!'

'For pity's sake, will you stop moaning! Anyway, it's all your fault! We've strayed so far off the beaten track, the natives don't even know what an omelette is!'

I was cold, hungry, brassed off and gagging on the stench that filled the car. 'You'd best stop that dirty animal from letting off or I swear I'll dump the pair of you on the side of the road!'

I'm not sure what it was that sent me into hysterics.

It could have been when Battersby fell off the seat, propelled by the longest, loudest rattle of escaping air I've ever heard; or it could have been Dickie's wide, frightened eyes.

Then again it could have been his glowing, bulbous ear, or the two of them whining and complaining and Dickie going on about the damned omlette! Anyhow, for some reason I got caught by a fit of giggles and I could not stop.

Holding my breath, I drew the car on to the side of the road and scrambled out, laughing so much I could hardly stand. 'GET OUT!' I spluttered, falling to the ground, 'and leave the doors open.' That was the last thing I said before Battersby launched himself through the air and flattened me. And even while I fought him off, I couldn't stop laughing. In my minds' eye, I could see the bigger picture: the hairy, smelly monster straddled across me like some creature out of the swamp, Dickie tumbling out of the car, a bright red swelling on the side of his head growing by the minute, and me rolling about the ground, helpless with laughter, frantic to escape what was rapidly becoming the worst nightmare of my life.

What were we doing here anyway? How did I get into this mess? All I ever wanted was a quiet time on my own to gather my thoughts about my ex-wife, who doesn't want me but who doesn't want anyone else to have me. Then there's my psycho mother threatening to do away with herself. I ask you! What did I do to deserve it all?

Mother has been writing to me, and hot on the heels of her last letter was a long, heartfelt warning from my dad:

Stay away, son.

The woman's gone mad. The minute you step through that door she'll have you trapped and you'll never see daylight again. For your own sake, you should ignore her silly threats to do away herself. She's too selfish for that. In fact sometimes I'm tempted to do it for her! I might be jailed for life, but the way I see it, a life sentence without her would be like a holiday.

Look, I'm just saying … she'll try any means in her power to get you back in her clutches, just like she's got me.

I'll never know what I ever saw in the wicked

mare. Sorry, son, I know she's your mother, but she's a bad 'un! On the first date she got me so drunk I didn't know what I was doing … before I knew what was happening, she had me trousers down. The upshot was you, and that's how she trapped me. She's always had a nasty side to her, but the older she gets the worse she gets. She keeps a bread knife under the bed … says it's in case o' burglars; now I can't sleep for fear of losing my precious parts!

Just think on what I'm saying! Be on your guard, son.

Love you, Dad

Needless to say, my dad's letter had me shaking in my boots. Truth is, I was really nervous. For all I know, she could be watching the flat. Worse than that, she could team up with Laura and the two of them might kidnap me, strip me naked and tie me up in Antonio's cellar. I'd be totally helpless! They could do all kinds of terrifying things and I wouldn't be able to scream because they'll have stuffed a rag down my throat.

Dear Lord above, I'm a nervous wreck!

And now, if that wasn't enough to contend with, I've got a problem with Poppy. Lately she's become really clingy; all over me like a rash and giving me the goo-goo eyes. She definitely fancies me. Oh, I'll admit she's a lovely little thing, and I'm sure she'll make some boy very happy when she grows up, but it won't be me, so she'd best get that crazy thought out of her head straightaway! And another thing! I wish she'd be more careful with that damned hosepipe! The thing is, she can't seem to help herself.

I've threatened to sack her, and I've even given her a few lessons on hose control, but she still can't seem to get the hang of it. It's not like she's got control of the hose, it's more like the hose has got control of her. One time it lifted her clean off her feet, swung her about then chucked her in the feed bins. The poor little kittens thought it was a missile. They hid in their cages for six days!

I've decided! When I get back I'll give the job of hosing-down to somebody more capable. The lad who did it before her was just as useless. However he managed to get the hose-end stuck up a drainpipe, I will never know.

Worse than that, the elusive owner came to inspect the premises last week and ended up being caught in a freezing gush of water that shot him up in the air, skidded him across the yard and left him stranded in the muck heap.

So there I was, lying on the ground, still reeling from recent events and chuckling to myself. I looked at Dickie Manse and the hairy hound, and I suddenly thought of that song All By Myself. What a luxury *that* would be!

For now though, I could see the funny side of things.

'I'm glad you find it funny!' Dickie glared at me, before snapping at the mutt, 'GET BACK INSIDE THE CAR!'

For a minute Battersby looked really sorry for himself. There was a moment of wonderful silence when it seemed he would do his master's bidding. Then in slow motion he drew back his lips and showed his teeth. Vigorously shaking himself, he then stood up, proudly sauntered towards Dickie, slowly emitting a loud and hissing explosion that shook the ground like an earthquake under our feet.

'STAY AWAY, YOU FILTHY PIG!' I have never seen Dickie move so fast.

With me in hot pursuit, the two of us legged it up the street, screaming and shouting, while the mutt calmly got back into the car, where he stared as us though the back window, somewhat bemused and well proud of himself. 'I think I'll walk the rest of the way!' Dickie spluttered, trying hard not to laugh.

'I think I'll join you!' I declared sombrely, before we were both helpless with laughter again.

And you know what? For some ridiculous reason, I began to feel that this trip was might turn out all right after all.

Right now, I could really do with a hot shower and a warm bed, but I knew that it wouldn't be that easy. No doubt, knowing my luck, the hotel proprietor will turn us away. I'm worried how they'll react when they get a whiff of what's arrived on their doorstep!

And I can't *imagine* what they'll say if they clock the hairy mutt!

BLACKPOOL, LATER THAT NIGHT...

Dear Diary,

We arrived at the hotel sad and weary. Dickie had this bright idea, 'Get yourself booked in. Me and Battersby will be right behind, and nobody will ever know.'

'No way!' I was adamant, 'You're coming up to the desk with me. We'll take our chances.'

'Take a gander at that!' Dickie sneaked a look at the burly porter, 'We'll be on the end of his boot an' sailing out the door before you can say "Jack Robinson".'

'Is that right? And whose fault will it be if we have to sleep on the beach, eh? Who was it that smuggled himself and that hairy mutt into my car, eh? And why should I worry what happens to you, tell me that?'

'Because we're mates, that's why.' He put on that little boy lost face.

'All right! All right! Hide the mutt as best you can, while I check in.' I gave him a shove, 'Get on with it then!' (Honestly! He's like a light gone out!)

I waited until the two of them were out of sight, then I straightened my jacket, wiped my shoes on my trouser legs, sidestepped the porter and sauntered ever so casually to the desk.

'Yes, sir?' The long streak at the desk twitched his nose and looked me up and down, 'What can I do for you?'

I gave him my most winning smile, 'I booked a single room, but I'd prefer a double if you have one available.'

'Name?'

'Ben Buskin.'

After locating my name in his ledger he peered over his spectacles, 'Three nights, is it, sir?'

'That's it, yes.'

'Bed, breakfast and evening meal?'

'Yes.'

'So, you now wish to swap the single room for a double, is that right, sir?'

'That's right, yes.' Has he got cloth ears or what?

Once again he bent his head to the ledger, 'Mmm…' He flicked the pages back and forth, constantly chunnering under his breath, 'Mmm… Can't seem to…'

Suddenly he pounced on the page with his pen at the ready, 'You're very fortunate, sir. We do have a double room available, but it's one of our premium rooms, so you must understand it is more expensive than the previous room.'

'How much more?'

He was at it again, flicking the pages and chunnering, 'Mmm… Mmm, now let me see…'

Shifting his spectacles, he perused the page, 'The single was £50 per night, bed, breakfast and evening meal. The premium room is £105 per night.'

'One hundred and five pounds a night? GOOD GRIEF!' It took a minute to recover, 'Is there any room for negotiation on that?'

He gave a patronising little smile, 'None whatsoever ... sir.'

'So, how much is the dinner?' I was doing mental calculations.

'The evening meal is £30.'

'So, how much is breakfast?'

'Twenty pounds.' By now he had stopped calling me 'sir'. (Pompous swine!)

'Right! So, if I took the bedroom for three nights, room only, it would work out at £55 per night?' We were in the right territory now, so to speak.

''Fraid not, sir.' With obvious glee he went on to explain, 'We are *not* a boarding house. We do *not* do rooms only. This is a fine hotel with a reputation to uphold.

'So?'

'So, we have overheads to meet, and a reputation to which we aspire.' He twitched his nose again, 'I'm sure you understand?'

'What if I included breakfast then?'

'Mmm!' He stretched his neck as far as it would go, then he groaned, before saying, 'Well, yes we can sometimes do bed and breakfast ... but...' I did not care for the way he fixed his beady eyes on me, '...only for business persons, who travel from place to place in a hurry.'

'Well, that's all right then!' I gave a sigh of relief, 'That's absolutely fine!' I felt like I'd got one over on him, '*I*, my good man, am exactly that ... a "business person".'

Fumbling in my wallet, I took out one of the kennel cards, and casually slid it across the desk. Keeping my cool, I pointed it out:

BEN BUSKIN – MANAGER

DAISY KENNELS
BEDFORD

All creatures lovingly cared for.

I swear he gave a little snigger, 'I see.'

'Right then! So you will know that I am the very man, Ben Buskin, exactly like it says there.'

Suddenly, from the corner of my eye I saw Dickie and the hairy mutt streaking across the foyer and out the back door. The porter must have taken a break. 'Good grief!' Grabbing a hankie out of his top pocket, the receptionist slapped it over his nose, just as the door slammed behind them, 'Whatever was that?'

'What?' I feigned innocence.

'That … THING!' Taking a deep breath he almost choked on the lingering vapour, 'Heavens above!' He made a face, 'Can't you smell it?'

I managed to keep a straight face, 'Can't say I do, no. But I really am anxious to get to my room. I've had a long drive, so if you don't mind, I need to get settled.' I even managed to sound irritated.

'Mmm.' He perused my business card once more, 'I'm not altogether sure we can accommodate you…'

'Well, I'm not altogether happy with your attitude,' I announced grandly. 'I'd like to speak with the manager.'

His manner changed instantly. He cleared his throat and he chunnered for a time, and then he spoke.

'I'm sure there's no need to be hasty. There's no reason to trouble the manager,' he assured me. 'You're right. Your card does seem to be in order, and the room is definitely booked, so yes, we can do the three nights for $55 per night.'

He must have had a previous upset with the manager, because he kept looking nervously towards the office door.

Either that or he was still puzzling over the hairy blur and the smell that had assulted his senses.

I was unpacking when there came a nervous knock on the door. 'Who's there?'

'Room service … sir.'

I recognised the rank smell emanating under the door. It was Dickie Manse brains-in-his-pants, and he sounded really brassed off.

'Phaw!' As I flung open the door, the pong enveloped me, 'Quick! Get in here, the pair of you!' As they came in, I glanced up and down the corridor. I was not surprised to see that it was empty.

'The smell's getting worse!' Dickie was green around the gills, 'When he fell down the ditch, Battersby must have landed on a dead rat.'

'You and him both!' I'm not joshing. I have never smelled anything like it in the whole of my life.

'We'll have to give him a bath or something.' Dickie was beginning to panic, 'If anybody comes in here, there'll be trouble.'

'Huh! *Sick* more like!' I tried to keep my distance but the rancid smell filled the room, 'Best open the windows before we choke to death!' While Dickie struggled the dog into the bathroom, I threw open all the windows.

It took all our strength and more to get the mountainous bulk washed. First we tried to lift him over the ridge, but he kept slithering back. Then we stood him up on his back legs and tried to shove him backwards. It was like the Krypton Factor! At one point we had one of his front legs over the rim and the rest of him sitting on the toilet.

We grappled and fought and the more we tried, the more tangled we got; it was only a matter of time before the giggling started.

It got even more uproarious when Dickie pretended that we were Dick and Dom, shifting a sofa, 'Me to you,' he kept saying, and I found myself replying, 'No, no, you to me.'

In the end we collapsed on the floor, exhausted and laughing while the mutt calmly strolled into the shower and stood there, regarding the two of us with a pathetic look. 'Look at that! He wants a shower,' I felt like a proud mother.

'He wants *drowning*, that's what he wants!' Dickie announced, and the mutt promptly cocked his leg and peed up the shower panel.

'FILTHY PIG!' One thing about Dickie; he has a way with words.

The next hour was pandemonium.

We all had a shower: me, Dickie, the bathroom, and the mutt. As for the shower curtain, it looked like it had been shredded with a cheese grater.

We were soaked, exhausted and in need of sustenance, but we did smell a good deal sweeter though.

Leaving the mess for the morning, we fell asleep in our respective places, with me in the double bed, Dickie Manse brains-in-his-pants on the sofa, and the mutt stretched out on the carpet.

What a day!

What a night!

So, what's next?

I thought of Rhett Butler's prophetic words in *Gone with the Wind*, 'Tomorrow is another day.'

I can't help wondering what joys it might have in store for us!

BLACKPOOL
SPETEMBER, SUNDAY

Well, diary! Here we are in Blackpool!

After a good night's sleep, I scrambled out of bed like an excited kid, flung back the curtains and threw open the windows. The wind took hold of the windows and wrenched them out of my hands, 'Good grief! It's like all hell let loose out there!'

'Mind your wig doesn't blow away!' Lazing on the sofa, Dickie Manse laughed as I struggled to shut the windows, 'I've heard how the weather in Blackpool can turn at the drop of a hat … sunny one minute, gale force the next.'

'Shut up you, I don't need a weather forecast.' He really gets my goat sometimes! 'I need to grab these windows before they take off. Don't help me though, whatever you do.' By now the windows were in a frenzy, crashing about and ready to take off at any minute.

Waiting for them to swing back in my direction, I leaned

over the window ledge, arms out, all set to grab the windows. 'Some holiday this is turning out to be!' I was fed up, sick of him and his stinking dog, and then to top it all, just as the windows came within reach, the hairy hound leaped on my back and launched me to the elements. Before I knew what was happening I was outside, clinging on to the window by the tips of my fingers; freezing buttocks bared to all and sundry and me screaming like a banshee. 'DICKIE! GET UP … DICKIE!' I could hardly hold on, 'DICKIE!'

'Stop panicking, you big girl's blouse, you'll do yourself a mischief! We're three floors up and there's a concrete car park down there.' He was really enjoying himself, 'One wrong move and you'll be splattered like an omelette.'

Deliberately taking his time he sauntered across the room, a sheet wrapped loosely round his middle, his hair standing up like the bristles of a brush. I don't know what was more frightening … the thought of putting my life in the hands of an idiot like Dickie Manse brains-in-his-pants, or hanging on to the window by the tips of my fingers; being whipped back and forwards, while the wind whistled a tune round my nether regions.

Suddenly my jim-jams got snatched away in a fierce gust of wind. I started screaming, 'HURRY UP! DEAR LORD, I CAN'T STAND MUCH MORE!' By now I was swinging half-naked, and so cold I couldn't feel a thing.

'OH, YOU POOR SOUL, DON'T DO IT! DON'T JUMP!' Some woman shouted from below, 'HE'S LISTENING, DEAR! WE ALL KNOW HOW HARD LIFE CAN BE AT TIMES, BUT YOU'RE NOT ALONE. HE UNDER-STANDS.'

Silly mare! 'IF HE'S LISTENING, HE MUST KNOW I'M FROZEN TO THE BONE AND ABOUT TO BE MANGLED! DOES HE UNDERSTAND THAT?'

'Hey!' Dickie was hanging out the window, 'How am I supposed to pull you in if you keep moving?'

'Pull the *window* in, you idiot!' I screamed. What's he like? 'In case you've forgotten, I'm on the end of it!'

'Right then, here we go. You swing the window in towards me and I'll grab you.' he glanced at my hands and other shrivelled bits. 'Trouble is,' he sniggered, 'I'm not sure which bit to grab!'

'When I get inside I'll wipe the smile off your face, you see if I don't!'

Suddenly, with alarming courage, Dickie threw himself across the window ledge, arms outstretched ready to help me back in. He might well have succeeded if only the big, hairy mutt hadn't got excited and sunk his teeth into Dickie's rear end. With a shriek of absolute terror, Dickie shot out the window, and got caught up by his towel, which attached itself to the window handle. 'HELP!' I always knew he was useless, 'WE'RE GONERS, THE PAIR OF US … GONERS, I TELL YOU.'

189

So there we were, hanging out the window, me all but stark-naked with a sharp-eyed crow waiting to swoop down and pick off my juicy bits, and Dickie Manse brains-in-his-pants screaming about how he was 'TOO YOUNG TO DIE LIKE THIS!' Bolt upright on his back legs, the hairy hound stared at us out the window, a toothy grin on his face, and a river of slaver running down his chin, 'HELP ME! I'M BLEEDING!' Dickie yelled. 'I CAN FEEL IT, ALL HOT AND STICKY, RUNNING DOWN MY BACK!'

'Will you stop yelling!' I was well out of patience and now my lips were freezing together, 'It's not blood. It's the Baskerville hound slobbering on you. And you know what … I COULDN'T CARE LESS!'

Suddenly it was like the whole world had turned out to see the show. Some goofy bloke was taking pictures of my bare rump, and two girls were shouting obsenities that would have shamed a navvy. There were police sirens below and somebody banging on our room door, and before we could catch our breath, we were yanked back inside and ordered to get dressed by a big fella in uniform. I'm sure we'd have got off with a warning, but Dickie got stroppy and we were then marched to a waiting police car. With Battersby strapped securely in the front seat and me in between Dickie and an officer in the back, we found ourselves being despatched at speed to the local cop shop; full sirens and everything!

As we went down the street, with all our worldly

belongings, we could hear the crowd laughing behind us; except for the woman shouting … 'HE'S UP THERE WATCHING! HE'LL HELP YOU, DEAR … DON'T YOU WORRY!' Dopey mare, what's she on?

At the station it took us a full hour to explain before we were let loose with a caution. 'Blackpool never wants to set eyes on you again!' The officer warned, 'So be off, and mind you keep your nose clean from now on.' I've no idea why he gave Battersby that shrivelling look, but it must have annoyed the mutt because as we left, he not only cocked his leg up the front door, he also left his calling card halfway down the steps. (I must give him a pep talk. This can't go on.)

'We'd better leg it outta here!' After that ordeal, Dickie was close to tears, 'I'm all for getting in the car and taking off.'

'What!' No way, I thought. 'We've come here for a good time, and I am not leaving yet!'

Now that we were far enough away from the police station I was fighting fit and ready for anything. I told Dickie, 'What's the world coming to when a couple of hard-working guys can't have a quiet weekend away without being arrested for disturbing the Queen's peace.'

As usual, Dickie showed his ignorance, 'What's that supposed to mean?'

'I am just saying that's why we got arrested … for disturbing the Queen's peace…'

'Well it weren't me! I never even *touched* her piece. I've got more respect than that. And what would my gran have said?'

All I could do was stare at him, 'What are you talking about?' Sometimes he's on another planet altogether.

Now he was totally confused, 'I'm talking about … what you just said…'

'Forget it. All I'm saying is, I am not being railroaded out of town for no one! We came here to have a good time, and that's what we're gonna have!'

'Are we?'

'Of course!' After all, I'm in charge.

'So we're really staying then?'

'Absolutely!'

'So … where are we gonna sleep?' Dickie had a point. The hotel manager had made it clear we weren't welcome back.

'Wherever we lay our head, that's where!'

'What … like Clint Eastwood in that film?'

'What film?'

'Can't remember now, but we need to find somewhere warm. If we sleep outside, we'll freeze!'

'Not while we've got Battersby we won't.'

'I'd rather freeze than fall asleep with a hairy dog lolloping all over me! Anyway, I'm hungry, and so is he. We didn't get our dinner.'

'What d'you fancy?'

192

He twitched his nose in the air, 'I can smell fish and chips.'

'Me too!' My stomach was playing a tune, 'Fish and chips it is then.'

I'd already noticed there seemed to be a fish and chip shop on every street corner, so it didn't take us long to find one. It was a small place that was warm and cosy; the proprietor was built like an outhouse while his daughter was small, pretty and *very* friendly. 'I like her.' Dickie was drooling more than the mutt.

'Keep your hands to yourself!' I whispered a warning, 'You can see the size of her dad, and we don't want to end up at the police station again, do we, eh?'

'No.'

'Good!'

So we tucked in, thawed out, and cheered up when the proprietor told us, 'The weather's taking a turn for the better tomorrow. I reckon we're in for a sunny spell.'

He heard our sorry story and offered us a room in the attic for a fiver a night, breakfast thrown in. 'You're on!' I couldn't believe it! Our luck seemed to be changing for the better.

Things were looking up at last. Everything was falling into place. We hadn't spent a penny; we were all intact (in *every* way, which was surprising!). We had not been formerly charged by the police, we had found ourselves a place to stay, and thanks to the generosity of the big man, we weren't about to starve.

Ironic though, how we ended up in a chippie … again!
How could we go wrong?

BLACKPOOL
SEPTEMBER, SUNDAY NIGHT

After a meal of the best fish and chips I've ever tasted, we were shown to our room, 'It's all I've got, but it's yours if you want it.' With the big man straddling the door, the light was shut out and for the first time in my life, I felt claustrophobic, 'There's no window.' I noticed that straightaway, 'Why is there no window?'

'It's a storage room.' When he eyed me up and down, I was reminded of Anthony Hopkins in that film *The Silence of the Lambs*. He cooked his victims and, after eating them, finished off with a glass of wine. (I was sure the big man fancied me as a lamb chop.)

I could see Dickie Manse was thinking the same, because he was swallowing convulsively. 'I would like a window,' he gulped, 'I might need to look out.'

What? I might need to *escape*! Never mind look out!

'Do you want it or not?' Cripes! The big fella was licking his lips now!

'Er … can you just give us a minute … please?'

'Why's that?'

'I'd like to have a little chat with my mate here … if that's all right?'

'I haven't got time for this!' he bellowed. (I didn't know he was a bellower, it was really unnerving.) 'Either you want the room or you don't…' he growled, '…one way or the other, it makes no difference to me.'

'A minute … please?'

'All right then! One minute, and that's it.'

I waited for him to go, but he stood firm. 'Right,' I edged away, taking Dickie Manse with me.

In a lowered tone I asked him what he thought we should do.

'Get the hell outta here … fast as we can!' In the flickering half-light, his eyes were like cracked plates.

'We've nowhere else to stay though.'

'I want to go home.'

'I've already told you … I am *not* going home!'

'I'll sleep on the beach then.'

'It's freezing out there!'

'I'd rather freeze than have my throat cut when I'm asleep!' His eyes swivelled towards the big man, 'I wasn't born to be barbecued neither!'

'He scares me too, but I have a plan.'

'What plan?'

'One that will protect us. So, are you with me or not?'

'Only if you promise to keep me and Battersby safe.'

'I will.'

'Promise then!'

'All right! I promise, is that good enough?'

When he nodded reluctantly, I lost no time in accepting. 'Right, we'll take it,' I told the big man. 'Thank you.'

Holding out his hand, he fixed his black eyes on me.

'He wants his fiver,' Dickie whispered in my ear. 'Give him it, and he'll go away.'

Fishing a five pound note out of my pocket, I gave it to him, and just as Dickie said, he went away, but not before eyeing us with a sly, furtive smile, 'Sleep well.' He chuckled and was gone.

'Did you see that!' Dickie was frantic, 'He means to kill us! He'll creep in here when we're fast asleep. He'll have us for breakfast. Look at Battersby … he knows what's up. He senses these things.'

He was right. The hairy mutt was quaking and shivering; his big eyes stared up at us, a look of desperation on his face.

I felt really sorry for him, 'It's all right, Battersby,' I leaned down to stroke him. 'The nasty man won't be able to get in, because I intend to barricade the door.'

We soon discovered he wasn't afraid of the big, bad man. Instead he was desperate to go to the loo, and now it was too late, because the floor was awash, and I was standing in it. 'Get away from me, you dirty animal!'

'You leave him alone!' Dickie made a beeline straight for me; then he went skidding across the floor to smack head-first into the wall. 'There's a leak!' he yelled, 'The whole place is under water!'

'It's not a leak, you dope. It's that hairy mutt, and his disgusting habits. We can't sleep here … not in that lot!'

'Filthy beast!' Dickie shook his head so hard it seemed like his hair had slid all to one side. 'Filthy, filthy creature! I've a good mind to put you in a home for unwanted dogs!' He didn't expect Battersby to leap on him, but he did, and the pair of them slid along the wall in a river of urine.

As if that wasn't enough, as Dickie staggered to his feet, the wall opened up and a big iron bed sprung out and squashed them flat. It was the strangest, most frightening thing I've ever seen.

And now the big man was at the door again, 'I forgot to tell you…' he gawped at the bed, with half a dog and Dickie's twisted leg sticking out from under it. 'Oh, you found it then,' he grinned, 'Sleep tight … mind the bed bugs don't bite.'

As he departed, he grumbled. 'There's a real smell of damp. I'll need to get that seen to.'

He slunk off, leaving chaos and destruction in his wake. 'The man's a psychopath!' Dickie squirmed out from beneath a ton of iron, 'He wants locking up!'

'And your dog wants plugging!' I told him straight, 'I don't care how you do it, but you'd best clean up the floor.' I'd seen a pile of old rags in the corner, 'Use some of that stuff there. After what the big man said, I'd best check the bed for bugs.'

There were no bugs; just a few holes in the mattress, with little mountains of escaped stuffing here and there.

Dickie used the old rags to wipe the floor; only to realise they were old blankets, obviously meant for us, because we searched every nook and cranny of the room, and found nothing but old beer cans and planks of wood in the corner holding up the ceiling. 'That's it! I'm going home!' Dickie wailed, 'I hate Blackpool, it's been one disaster after another!'

Fed up with his whining, I had a go. 'Oh, yes … blame Blackpool, that's it! And whose fault is it really, eh? Who snuck into my car when all I wanted was a quiet weekend, away from you and that dirty animal.'

'Well, I'm sorry, Ben … but me and Battersby are going home, and that's that!'

'So, it's all about you again, is it? You selfish article!'

'We're leaving and nothing you can do or say will make me change my mind!'

'Fair enough, go then! But you'll have to go on the train, because I'm staying here. Tomorrow, I mean to have a good day, and nothing you or the mutt can do will stop me enjoying myself. Have you got that?'

'We can't go on the train.'

'Oh, and why's that?'

'Because, if we go on the train, they'll probably put Battersby in the guard's van.'

'Good! Then he can't cause havoc in the carriages.'

'It might smell in the guard's van.'

'It'll smell even more when the mutt gets in there!'

'I'm not going on the train.'

'So, what *are* you going to do?'

'Aw look, Ben. Can't we find somewhere else, then. Please?'

'There is nowhere else, as well you know.'

'Anywhere's better than here! There's something wrong with that bloke, and you know it.' He glanced furtively at the door. 'Did you see how he looked at us?'

'So?'

'Didn't you think he was creepy?'

'Maybe.'

'If me and Battersby stay, do you think the big man might sneak into the room while we're asleep?'

'Okay! Yes, his *is* creepy, and yes, *it is* possible he might sneak into the room while we're asleep, but we're in Blackpool … capital of fun. *Anything's* possible!'

'He frightens me.'

'Why does that not surprise me? A kid on a toy scooter would frighten you! Besides, we've got the mutt to protect us.'

'What! He'd be more frightened than us. *You* said you would protect us.'

'And I will.'

'So, how do you mean to do that?'

'Well ... I thought if we left the door open, and he came after us, we could make our getaway.'

'But if he came after us, he'd shut the door behind him ... probably lock it too.' His eyes popped out of his head. 'We'd be at his mercy!'

'Hmm...' I must admit, I hadn't thought of that. 'Okay, but if we left here, the only place to sleep would be the beach. We can't sleep in the car, because we left it at the hotel and I don't fancy walking back there. Besides, it'll be damned freezing in the car, and damned freezing on the beach!'

'Battersby would keep us warm.'

'Yes, and wet, and his fleas would keep us scratching all night!'

In fact, the prospect of sleeping with Battersby was horrific. 'What makes you think I want to be smothered to death, or peed on from a great height, or worse still, have a slobbery tongue all over me!' (Mind you, I suppose it depends who the tongue belongs to.)

'Please, Ben! Let's get out of here!'

'NO!'

'All right. You stay here and be murdered in your bed. Me and Battersby are off to sleep on the beach.'

I watched him collect his bits and pieces, before lolloping out of the room, with Battersby sloping behind.

When I heard the front door shut, I watched through a crack in the wall, and there they were … going down the street, a real sorry pair.

'Go on then … clear off, and the best of luck to you!' Dickie was right, the place was a real dump, but it had to be better than sleeping rough in the cold.

By now I was in a foul mood, 'Scaredy-cat Dickie!' Frightened of the big man because he thought he looked at him in a funny way. Mind you, who wouldn't look at Dickie Manse brains-in-his-pants. I mean, just look at the state of him! I've never been able to make head nor tail of him neither!

I muttered and moaned as I curled up on the corner of the bed, 'Go and sleep on the beach then, and take the hairy monster with you, see if I care!' In half an hour I reckoned he'd be back with his tail between his legs!

The idea of the pair of them creeping back through the door and Dickie grovelling apologies, made me smile. Oh, yes! They'll be back all right, but I wasn't going to let them in … well, not until I'd made them suffer for their treachery.

I hated him. I hated myself, and as the minutes ticked away and still he didn't return, I got more and more uncomfortable. I was determined not to go after him. This was my holiday and he'd ruined it. I was not about to let him dictate the terms of what time was left. No way!

Murdered in my bed. What an imagination he had. Then a shiver went through me. What if he was right? Naw! He was just peeved because we'd been thrown out of the hotel. Anyway, what had he got against the big man? For all we knew he might be the softest, gentlest creature on earth.

But the more I thought of the big man, and what Dickie has said, the more I was on edge. Why would he want to come into our room in the middle of the night? I reassured myself, 'He's done nothing for us to be worried about. In fact, he's been really kind ... letting us stay here when he doesn't know us from Adam. And besides, who else would have let a mutt like Battersby into their house?'

The thought of the dog made me homesick. He's accident prone. He stinks to high heaven, and when his rear end gets talking, it's like thunder and lightening all at once.

Actually, when I got to thinking and wondering, and asking myself why the big man even let us through the door, I began to wonder if Dickie Manse brains-in-his-pants, wasn't right after all.

Feeling a fool for letting myself believe the ranting of a bloke like Dickie, I laughed out loud. Snuggling down I was determined to ignore his warning.

Actually, to tell the truth, the bed wasn't too bad once I'd got settled. Fully dressed, and with some of my clothes thrown over me, I felt myself nodding off. 'At least I'm warm,' I told myself. 'At least I'm not shivering on a cold, lonely beach.'

I don't know what time it was when I woke, but I was freezing cold. 'What's that?' Someone was touching my leg. I had visions of myself and the big man's pretty daughter, rolling about the bed, getting to know each other, and was I thankful that Dickie Manse brains-in-his-pants was not here? You bet!

There it was again … all soft and smooth against my leg, 'Stop it … you're giving me goose bumps!' By now I was sniggering like a silly boy. It was just like the day I got Julie Tumble in the bike shed at school.

There it was again … velvet-soft against my leg, giving me goose bumps, 'You naughty … *naughty* girl.' I couldn't see anything in the dark, but she was snuggling up to me and it was all too much, 'Come on then!' I felt well pleased with myself, 'If you want me … *take* me. I'll never be more ready than I am now!'

When the touch of her soft skin slid up my thigh, I knew I was in for a real treat. In fact I hadn't been that excited since I slept with that woman I picked up and got kicked out of house and home as punishment.

Worried that the excitement might wear off, I held out my hand and slowly raised my head, 'That's enough of the teasing, why don't we just get to it!'

She was on my neck now, all soft and cuddly, the wispy fringes of her hair tickling my face, 'That's enough!' I was beside myself. 'Take me now!'

Determined to steal a peep, I looked up, straight into the eyes of the biggest rat I'd ever seen. Then I realised they were all over me; dozens of beady eyes staring back at me, their needle sharp teeth ready to strike. Screaming like a lunatic, I leaped up and ran, 'Aaagh! Where are you, Dickie!'

They must have heard my screams in Timbuktu, 'Get 'em off, Get 'em off!' I was running about in panic, when the big man burst into the room. 'What are you doing to my daughter? Don't deny it … I heard you telling her to "get 'em off". I'm warning you … if you're not out that door in two minutes flat, I'll break every bone in your body!'

Busy thrashing me with a yard broom, he didn't think where his daughter might be, or Dickie, nor did he see the rats as they scurried into the shadows. He launched himself at me, like a man demented, 'Dirty pervert! I knew you were trouble the minute I clapped eyes on yer!'

Fearing for my life, I grabbed my bag and ran, falling and tripping all the way down the street. 'Dickie!' I was panic-stricken. '*Dickie*! Where the hell are you?'

I could see the daughter peering at me out of a window, but there was no sign of Dickie, the deserter. The big man must have been a champion javelin thrower, because the broom came whistling through the air like a jet-propelled rocket. Catching me square in the back of the neck, it threw me at speed along the promenade, before momentum had me over the wall and on to the beach.

Bent and broken, I lay there, in the dark, on my own, without a friendly soul in the world.

In that sorry moment of mayhem, with my brain still reeling, Dickie and his hairy mutt seemed like the best mates a man could ever have.

'I've got to find them!' I told myself, 'If I have to search every inch of this beach and every street in Blackpool, I will find them!'

After catching my breath, I gathered myself together and felt the damage: a torn right ear, a bruise on my nether regions, and trousers I couldn't keep up because I'd fled without my belt.

Dejected and lonely, I kept a tight hold on my pants, and began my way along the beach.

Where would Dickie have gone? I looked left and I looked right, and then I looked again, and all I could see were endless miles of beach; all I could hear was a couple making love noisily under the pier, and a mangy dog howling for a mate. From somewhere in the distance came the sound of hearty laughter, and all along the promenade the colourful lights danced and twinkled.

Suddenly it was like all my troubles melted away. With the carnival lights illuminating the night skies, the comforting feel of sand squashing under my feet, and the tangy smell of the sea in my nostrils, I believed that Blackpool might still turn out to be every bit as magical as I'd imagined.

After a few hundred yards, I heard the music and with lighter heart, I began trudging towards it. 'Here I am, Dickie!' I shouted to the elements. 'You've been a good friend to me, and I've never needed you more than I do now!'

'Bugger off, gobbie!' A man yelled out of the blue. 'You find your Dickie and leave the rest of us in peace!' Then I heard a girl's voice giggling, 'Ooh, Monty, you've never touched me there before. You can do it again if you like.'

I didn't need to guess what they were up to, but it made me think. 'All right, Dickie,' I chuckled, 'we came to Blackpool to have fun, and that's what we'll do … all of us, you, me and the hairy mutt!'

SOME TIME LATER...

I must have walked for ages. My feet ached, my back hurt, and my throat was dry as paper. But I wasn't going to give in. I kept going; the twinkling lights were never far behind me, and in front the beach stretched on forever.

After a while trudging along, I dropped, exhausted, into the sand. I didn't try and get up. Instead I just lay there, stretched out, every inch of my poor, battered body aching. I knew exactly what John Mills felt like in that film *Ice Cold in Alex*.

I must have been lying there for a good ten minutes or even longer, when I heard singing. 'Alice … Alice… Who the hell is Alice…' It was rowdy and cheeky, and though I couldn't be sure, I thought I recognised Dickie's voice. I thought it might be him, because nobody else could be so out of tune.

Clambering up, I yelled out, 'Dickie! You were right; I should have left when you did! There were rats everywhere … in the bed … eyeing me up, gnawing at my bits and pieces! Listen, Dickie … it's me! It's Ben! I've come to find you!'

When the singing stopped, I waited a while, then I shouted again, and still nothing. Then I heard a soft, wooshing noise and before I could look round, I was brutally wrestled to the ground. Then I recognised the smell.

'Get off, you stinking mutt!' Shoving Battersby aside, I looked up and I thought I'd gone to heaven, because right there before me were two angels, each with long hair and dressed skimpily.

They reached out to help me up, and then Dickie was there. 'I knew you'd find me,' he said cockily, 'I said you'd be along soon, and here you are.'

After a swift introduction, we walked back along the promenade; Dickie arm in arm with the dark-haired girl called Frankie, and me all wrapped round Joanna, the blonde. 'So, you managed to find a hotel that would take you in, eh?' I was well chuffed.

'Not exactly a hotel,' he answered.

'Oh? So, if not a hotel … what?'

A few minutes later I found out.

It was a two-berth camper van parked near the promenade, it was not even big enough to swing a cat in, which meant Battersby was in your face and you could hardly turn over. *That was the downside*.

The upside was that Battersby could be tied up outside, to the rear end of the camper van while the rest of us stayed inside, nice and cosy, which meant that we could all get to know each other very well.

Dickie and Frankie went away to the front of the camper van, shutting the curtains behind them, while me and Joanna retreated towards the back. 'I do like you, Ben.' She had the sweetest voice.

'You don't even know me.' Though with a bit of luck and careful handling, we could soon put that right, I thought hopefully.

'I still like you.'

'Ah, well, that's good. So now we know each other's names and we like each other. That can't be bad, can it, eh.' Honestly! How lame was that for an opening bid?

'Ben?'

'Yes?'

'Are you married?' She was making cow-eyes at me, but I didn't care. Wow! She had such beautiful eyes, all shimmery and dark brown and kinda mesmerising.

'Ben?'

'Yup?'

'Are you…?' she hesitated.

'Am I what?'

'Are you married?' she asked again.

'Nope!' Saying that felt really good. Okay, I know! After Laura, I said never again, but who knows? For the right woman, I might be tempted to bite the bullet. In fact, there was a moment when I even thought of taking little Poppy out on a date, but she was bit young for me really.

'So, have you got a girlfriend?' Boldly flashing her cleavage, Joanna had my full attention.

'No girlfriend!' That was some cleavage! Honest to God, it was like the Swiss Alps down there!

'Are you gay?'

'Not as far as I'm aware. Nope!'

'So you're free and easy?'

'Yup! Easy as they come.'

'D'you like me?'

'Sure do!'

'You sound like Johnny Cash.'

'Is that good or bad?'

'It would have been good if he'd been younger, but he's old now.'

'I see.' I decided not to tell her Johnny Cash was actually dead.

'Can you sing?'

'Nope.'

'Johnny Cash sings good. I like his songs, but I don't like old men.'

'I don't blame you.' She wouldn't like dead men, either!

'So you see, Ben? Hey! That is your *real* name, isn't it?'

'Unfortunately, yes. Although if I'd been given the choice, it would have been something else.'

'Like what?'

'I don't know. I didn't get the choice, did I?'

'Aw, go on! What name would you have liked ... if you'd had the choice that is?'

'Dunno.' I gave a shrug, just to let her know I was not about to be drawn into her silly game. Like all women she was out to humiliate me!

'You're not being nice to me, Ben.'

She was turning on the sulks like they all do!

'Shall I guess what name you would have chosen?'

'You can if you like, but you'll never guess.'

'Thomas?'

'No.'

'Jack?'

'No.'

'What then?'

'I'm not telling. You'll only laugh.'

'I won't! She made the sign. 'Cross my heart and hope to die!'

'Oh, all right then!'

'So, go on then … what name would you have chosen?'

I cleared my throat, 'Duke!'

Her eyes nearly popped out of her head. '*Duke!*'

'Yes … Duke!'

'So, what's your surname?'

'Buskin.'

'Huh!'

'What's with the "huh"?'

'I was just thinking, that's all.' She looked up at the ceiling. 'Duke … Buskin.' She began to giggle. 'Duke Buskin … *Duke Buskin*, it sounds really funny!' And then she was laughing out loud, rocking back and forth.

'I though you said you wouldn't laugh!'

'I lied!'

She sat up and I turned away in disgust. 'Oh, Ben, I'm sorry, I didn't mean to laugh, and anyway your real name is so much nicer … Ben Buskin, yes, it's got a real strong ring to it.'

She had me now. 'Do you really think so?'

'I do, yes.'

'Thank you. No one's ever said that before.'

'Ben?'

'Yes?'

'Do you really like me? I mean … *really*!'

I looked her up and down. 'Well, yes, of course I do.' Play it cool, Ben, I told myself. Don't be too eager. She's like all women. If you show too much interest, she'll have you.

'I like you too.' I reckon she'd had her teeth whitened, because when she smiled, I could see myself in her canines.

'That's nice to know,' But be careful, Ben! Let a woman see you're keen, and she'll have you tied up and under her thumb before you even know it. Look at my ex! No thank you! I've been there, done that; and I do not want to be doing it again!

'Ben?'

'Yes?'

'Would you like to go to bed?'

'I'm not sure. I mean, I'm not ready to go to sleep just yet.' I had other things on my mind.

'NO!' She gave a loud sigh. 'I didn't mean *that*!'

'What *did* you mean then?'

'I meant … would you like to go to bed … *with me*?'

There really was no answer to that, except to nod and hope for the best.

'Lead on!' I managed to keep my voice calm and matter of fact, when all the time I wanted to punch my fist in the air and yell so loud that my ex would hear me, and anyone else who doubted that I could ever again get myself a decent girl!

I managed to stay cool, when all the time I wanted to run and leap. Only the way things were it might have been a bit painful.

'Come on then, big boy.' She took my hand and we

213

climbed up to the cabin, where she told me not to worry about my missing trouser belt (which was a blatant invite if ever I've heard one!).

Just as we were getting settled, pandemonium broke out!

First, music exploded from the front of the van, and then Battersby was barking like mad. 'Hey you two ... whatever you're up to, leave it for now!' Dickie shouted up. 'Get yourselves down here! There's a party kicking off!'

Cut off just as I was getting somewhere, I scampered off the bed and led Joanna to the front of the van. 'We were just getting to know each other!' I moaned at Dickie. 'What's going on?'

When he grandly stepped aside, I saw why they'd pulled the curtains shut. It was a surprise. The sofa was laid with a cloth and spread with all kinds of goodies: cream crackers and dips, a plate of cheese straws, little sausage rolls, and other titbits, all laid out and backed up with bottles of drink. 'Where did you get all that?' It was amazing.

'We're always ready for a party!' That was Frankie. 'Me and Joanna, we're free spirits. We go where we like, do what we like, and we can stop anywhere, cos we've got wheels and we've got music!' And to illustrate her point, she turned the sound up full volume, and it all kicked off. All the sixties and seventies hits: the Rolling Stones, Elvis the pelvis, and other good stuff, which makes you want to jump about, even if you'd rather be doing something else.

In the background, Battersby was barking and whining so much, I had to lean out the van and tell him in no uncertain terms to be quiet. He promptly cocked his leg in my direction and christened the towbar. 'You can stay there,' I told him, 'until you learn how to behave!' Now I was in the mood to party!

From outside it must have seemed like an earthquake was happening in the van.

The music was loud and frantic, and the four of us were up on our feet, dancing like there was no tomorrow. Outside, Battersby was howling like a werewolf and the van was rocking form side to side like a boat on the ocean, which was a bit worrying because we were on a slope.

In the middle of all this frenzy, no one realised that the handbrake had worked itself loose.

Suddenly we were all thrown to the floor, and Dickie Manse brains-in-his-pants was screaming like a girl, 'BLOODY HELL! THE CAMPER VAN'S ON THE MOVE!'

I looked out the window and saw Battersby, tied to the back of the van, wide-eyed and terrified, and running so fast, I'm surprised he didn't take off!

'Hold on, Battersby!' I shouted, but the poor little bugger couldn't really do anything else but hold on, could he?

'I'll try and stop the van!' Dickie yelled at me. 'You see if you can reach out the window and free Battersby!'

I didn't need telling twice. If that poor mutt wasn't soon freed, he'd end up padless; maybe even legless.

'Hold my legs while I lean out!' I instructed Joanna, who by then was beginning to panic.

'We're all gonna die, aren't we?' she cried. 'Mam! I love you, Mam … and I'm sorry but it were me who ate the last of that cherry cake!'

'Never mind the damned cherry cake!' I told her, 'I'm going out the window. Hold on to my legs and don't let go!'

'You're going out the window?' All big eyed and shaking, she got hold of me. 'That's not a good idea. But if you're going, I'm going with you! That way we stand a better chance.'

'NO! You silly mare!' I'd gone right off her, 'I'm gonna save Battersby. He's tied to the back of the van and he can't stop running!'

'Oh, so you weren't trying to escape then?'

'LOOK! Just grab hold of my ankles. There's no way I can get him up here, but I might be able to untie the rope, then we can find him after we manage to stop the van.' By now it was rolling along at a terrifying pace.

The window was smaller than I had thought, and it was proving impossible to get my entire frame through it.

I managed to get my head and shoulders through without any trouble. Then I found I could squeeze my buttocks through, but then I got stuck good and proper. I was too far out to get back in, and not far enough out to reach poor Battersby. I felt awful. There he was, looking up at me with big, shocked eyes, his bark now little more than a pitiful whine, and his legs going so fast you couldn't make one from the other!

'Can you get him?' Joanna asked.

'No!'

'What d'you want me to do then?'

'Just hold on to me and whatever happens, don't let go!'

Taking a deep breath I breathed in and inched further out the window, but I still couldn't reach him. So I wiggled a bit more, and as I wiggled out, my trousers slipped back and the cool air rushed to my nether regions. 'Ooh! Look at you! I can see your bum!' Joanna was beside herself with excitement. 'You've got a really lovely bum!'

The silly mare! Didn't she know this was a crisis?

'D'you mind if I pinch it?'

'KEEP YOUR HANDS TO YOURSELF! Just hold on. And whatever you do … don't let go!' I was frantic because I was so far out, there seemed to be no way back. 'DICKIE! I can't get back … stop the pigging van will you!'

'I'M TRYING!'

'WELL TRY HARDER! AND TURN THAT DAMNED MUSIC OFF!'

'I'M BUSY TRYING TO STOP THE VAN! THE HAND-BRAKE'S LOCKED UP!'

'WHERE'S YOUR GIRLFRIEND?'

'SHE'S STEERING THE DAMNED THING! WHERE'S YOURS?'

'OGLING MY BUM!'

'WHAT DID YOU SAY?'

'I SAID … SHE'S GOT ME BY THE ANKLES, SO I DON'T FALL OUT!'

We seemed to be going faster and faster. The hairy mutt was barking like fury and the music got louder and louder, and now, in all the chaos, a police car was giving chase, it's siren blaring.

'Ooh, look!' That was Joanna. 'How exciting! We're being chased by the police. Wow! They'll never believe this … it's like a scene from Life on Mars.' Joanna squealed.

It was only later, when we were presented with a transcript of the officer's call-in to the station, that we had any idea what was going on in the police car:

OFFICER DAVE JACKSON: 'All units, we've got a run away camper van travelling at speeds of eighty miles an hour along the promenade. There seems to be loud music and lots of screaming and shouting coming from inside the van.'

OFFICER PARRY: 'Ooh, look! There's a hairy dog tied to the rear of the vehicle, and a half-naked bloke hanging out the window by his trousers. Move in quick, Dave! The buggers won't know what's hit 'em!'

OFFICER DAVE JACKSON: 'All units, we're
   closing in. Correction! The van is not
   stopping, I repeat, not stopping. It looks
   like they want to play – we're still in
   pursuit along the promenade. Switching
   lights and siren to full. This is it, Harry,
   first bust of the night coming up!'

Scared witless and still attached to the rear of the van,
Battersby was so desperate to escape he was in danger of
strangling himself.

Above him, I was frantic, frozen through and exposed
to all and sundry. Half in half out, I was being thrown from
side to side like a rag doll, screaming for Joanna to pull
me in. 'YOU STUPID MARE, I'M GETTING WHIPLASH!'

And then the rain began to pelt down, wetting my bits
and pieces, 'FOR GAWD'S SAKE ... WHAT'S WRONG
WITH YOU?' Now I was more frightened than angry.

Deaf to my pleas, Joanna was hopping about with excitement, craning her neck to see the pursuing police car. 'Look
at 'em go, Ben! Oh, I wish my mam could see this!'

We were approaching the traffic lights when it happened.
Dickie later told me that the driver approaching from the
opposite direction, who looked like he was having a sing
along to his radio music, saw us coming straight for him,
at full speed and out of control. He obviously panicked
and swerved violently to the right and ended up in a fish

and chip shop window, with the wooden sign through his windscreen saying: Cod and chips £2. Mushy peas thrown in.

The camper van then swerved to the left, did a bit of a jig, then tipped over a low wall and landed sideways on, on the beach.

Thrown on to the utility bed, Dickie said Joanna all but wet herself with excitement. 'We're beached! Look, Ben! We're beached, and there's me without me cossie!'

I couldn't look because when the van went over the wall I was released from the window, flew like a cannon ball and landed, hard, on the beach. I was told it was a while before I was found, trouser-less and all but unconscious, with the hairy mutt whining nearby. Luckily the mutt was still intact, thanks to the fact the rope tying him to the back of the van snapped on impact.

'You're nicked!' Before I knew what was happening, I was handcuffed and marched to the waiting police car. When the others finally staggered out of the van, they were arrested too. Squashed between Joanna and the hairy mutt I was past caring that I had been nicked for being naked in public. Again. Gawd, I hope the nosey gits back home don't get wind of it!

'Phaw!' Winding down the window, the policemen were looking a bit green. It was all I could do not to laugh as Battersby let rip another almighty fart. When I tried to explain to the officers I got short shrift.

'Shut it, you! You're in enough trouble as it is!' When he started caughing he couldn't stop. Well done Battersby dog!

When we arrived at the station, I was given an old coat to throw over my pride and glory. 'I want my pants!' I looked like a tramp and I was not having it.

'You'll get what you're given and be thankful!' That was the duty officer, a walrus in uniform, with two yellow, shifty eyes that moved in opposite directions.

He glared at the two officers who had nicked us, who, judging by the way they were grinning from ear to ear, were very proud of themselves. 'Officer Jackson and officer Parry, what've you got then?' The duty officer trained his shifty eyes on me and the others, 'looks like you've bagged a right motley crew here, an' no mistake.'

Dickie was hunched up and in pain, due to the fact he had been bent double for too long, trying to stop the runaway camper van. Frankie and Joanna were trying to chat up the duty officer, who froze them out with a hardened stare.

Battersby was a mangled mess, his big, terrified eyes swivelled from side to side, and I looked like a refugee from a war zone, with my chattering teeth and my hair standing to attention.

'Right then! What are we charging 'em with?'

Officer Jackson listed all the offences: 'Animal cruelty, breaking the speed limit, being a danger on the highway, indecent exposure, indirectly causing damage to a fish

221

and chip shop premises, endangering other drivers, failing to stop when pursued by the police, resisting arrest when handcuffed, abusing officers of the law when we were merely trying to execute our duty … and that one there … he pointed to Battersby, farted in our police car!'

'I see!' The walrus remained stalwart in his duty. 'Were they over the limit?'

'Not as far as we know.' Officer Jackson replied.

'What do you mean … not as far as you know? Did you breathalyse them?'

'We didn't have a breathalyser in the car.' Officer Parry piped up.

The walrus gave the him a shrivelling look, 'You'd best go and find one then, hadn't you?'

I saw my chance here, 'Excuse me, officer, but if you didn't breathalyse us when you first brought us in, doesn't that mean you can't do it now?'

Before the walrus could answer, officer Jackson bellowed in my ear, 'SHUT IT, YOU!' Not wanting to antagonise them further, I shut it quick.

Officer Parry came scuttling back, 'Somebody's gone and nicked it! I've looked everywhere and I can't find it!'

'Well, what about these two?' The duty officer stared over his bushy eyebrows at Joanna and Frankie, 'I have an idea we know these two from old, is that not the case?'

Officer Jackson agreed. 'I'd say they're probably at the root of it!'

All eyes were now trained on the two women, and because I was a gentleman at heart, I tried to defend them. 'It wasn't their fault, officer.'

Dickie butted in, 'It was all a mistake. Y'see … we met these ladies, then we went back to their camper van and we put on some music and we were just dancing, and then the handbrake shook loose and the van ran away with us.'

'It was an unfortunate accident…' I was really getting into my stride now, '…we were actually trying to rescue the situation, when these officers turned up like a pair of maniacs let loose! The siren sounded like a banshee from hell, and our poor dog was terrified!'

'We had it all in hand, then suddenly it was mayhem. There was me, hanging out the window trying to rescue the dog, but I was well and truly hooked up by my pants and couldn't go forwards or backwards. Worse still, when the van crashed, I shot out like a cork from a bottle and ended up on the beach all sick and dizzy. The poor man in the other car went through the chip shop window! As for poor Battersby, he's a shivering, frightened wreck. When he's frightened he farts, and when he farts it's just absolutely awful!'

'Mmm.' The walrus took a moment to consider, before questioning Dickie, 'So you were dancing, were you?'

'Yes, officer!' If you ask me, it was Dickie Manse brains-in-his-pants who caused all the trouble.

'What … in the camper van … all four of you?'

'Yes, sir.'

'And when you were dancing, didn't you realise the van was moving?'

'No, sir.'

'So, didn't any of you think about the consequences of all this dancing and shaking?'

'No, sir.'

'And the brake shook loose, is that what you're claiming?'

'Yes! I tried my best to pull it back on, but it got stuck. Then the van started careering out of control, and then these officers came along all noisy and everything, and oh, my back was really hurting, and it...'

I thought it was time to have my say, 'If you don't mind me saying, officer, it was as much these policemen's fault as ours...'

'SHUT IT!' Officers Jackson and Parry yelled in unison.

The walrus got all official, 'I see. So you had no knowledge of these two...' he pointed at Joanna and Frankie '...before you met them tonight?'

'None whatsoever.' I asserted my authority, 'I can assure you, officer, we are not in the habit of picking up women.'

The walrus glared at us one at a time, finishing up with me, 'Would you like to know what I think?'

'I would, yes. Thank you.'

'Well, for what it's worth, I think you've got too much to say for yourself.'

'Yes, officer.' I decided to say no more.

Gesturing to me, Dickie and the hairy mutt, the walrus told the officers to take us to the cells to cool off.

As we were being marched off, I looked back to see the walrus addressing the two women, 'Will you never learn?' he demanded, thumping his desk. 'Time and time again, you're brought before us, and it's always the same. You target the poor, lonely fools on the streets, then you take them back to that van of yours and ply them with drink. The poor sods think they're about to have the best time of their miserable lives, but when they're drunk you take everything they've got, then you throw them out on the streets, before driving off into the sunset.'

I could see him shaking his head. 'You really are a despicable pair. To my mind you need to be put away for a very long time. Who knows, this time we might just be able to accommodate you!'

Me and Dickie heard it all, and as we were thrown into the cell, we looked at each other with mouths open, too shocked and confused to take it all in.

We'd been taken in by a pair of thieves who preyed on men, took everything they had and then abandoned them.

That's exactly what Laura did to me! In fact, in my unhappy experience, it's what *every* woman does if they get the chance; use you up, squeeze you dry, then chuck you to the wolves!

All wound up and humiliated, I was ready for a fight,

and unfortunately Dickie Manse brains-in-his-pants was the nearest. 'It's all your fault! If you hadn't snuck into my car, I'd have been here on my own, away from you and that hairy, stinking mutt!'

From somewhere down the corridor, officer Parry yelled out, 'FOR ONCE AND FOR ALL … WILL YOU SHUT IT!'

Angered, I felt the need to defend myself and Dickie, so I yelled back, 'Excuse me, officer, but you've obviously made a mistake. These two women are not robbers! If they were, we would have sussed them straight off. Because, regardless of what you might think, we're not stupid enough to be taken in by two dumb women. I'll have you know we are sensible, intelligent blokes; and we have a great deal of experience when it comes to women.'

Dickie joined in, 'Yes, that's right! You obviously have no idea who you're messing with. My mate is the manager of a kennels. What's more, he knows a thing or two when it comes to women, and if he says you've got the wrong end of the stick, he knows what he's talking about!'

There was a long silence. Then all three officers bellowed out, 'SHUT IT!'

Miserable, cold and dejected, I sat in the cell, looking at the four walls and wondering how it had come to this, when all I wanted was a quiet weekend away by myself.

'I'm sorry I got us into this,' Dickie was genuinely sorry. 'D'you forgive me, Ben?'

'No.'

'But I really am sorry.'

'So you should be!'

'I really liked Frankie,' he sighed. 'I didn't know she was a professional thief.'

'We don't really know that for sure, do we?' I had my doubts. 'But if it is true, then we'll just have to put it down to experience!'

'You're very wise, Ben,' Dickie said humbly. 'I've always thought that.'

'Well, you either have it or you don't!'

'I don't like the idea of them keeping the girls back. For all we know those three could be having their wicked way with them.'

'Don't be so dramatic! Policemen don't do that sort of thing!'

'Well, I didn't like the look of that duty officer. And don't forget, officer Parry forgot the Breathalyser?'

'I wouldn't be at all surprised if they have to let us go because of that!'

'D'you reckon?' Dickie perked up.

As it turned out I was right. Some time later we were woken up. 'Come on, you two!' Officer Jackson threw open the cell door. 'Get outta here, before I change my mind!'

227

'Can we see the girls?' Dickie wanted to know.

'They've been released, but if I were you, I would clear off back to where you came from.' He gave me a hefty shove. 'Now go on the lot of you. Out!'

Before they let us leave, the walrus read us the riot act. 'This time, you were let off lightly. Next time, you may not be so lucky.'

The officers has organised the retrieval of the busted camper van. At the same time they had collected our belongings, which they handed to us. Fed up, tired and totally dejected, we made our way on to the street.

Dickie broke the silence as we emerged into bright sunshine. 'I reckon we had a lucky escape,' he said. 'I dread to think what might have happened if the van hadn't run away with us. The police saved us!'

I was miffed, 'So you think the police were right after all, and the girls really were dangerous robbers?'

'Sorry, Ben, I know you don't want to admit it,' Dickie answered, 'but I think we were taken in big time!'

I felt like the world's worst fool, 'This whole trip has been a disaster from start to finish. Come on, let's go and get the car and make our way back home.'

Dickie was having none of it, 'No way! All right, so we've been caught out and we should have known better. But at least we've escaped with our pride intact ... well, some of it, and we've still got the money we came with. The sun's shining and I'm starving. What say we have a big fried breakfast, play the amusement arcade and win big. *Then* we'll go get the car and head off home.'

I liked the idea. 'Okay, but on one condition.'

'What's that?'

'When we get back, not one word about this cock-up. All right?'

'Yes!'

'I mean it, Dickie ... not one word ... ever!'

'All right, yes. Look, right now I'm not thinking about women. I'm thinking about fried eggs, sausages, bacon and mushrooms ... oh, and a slice or two of toast.'

We were making for the pier in search of a café, when I suddenly remembered, 'Where's my mobile?' I frantically searched my pockets. 'I told Poppy to ring me if there was an emergency.'

'What kind of emergency?'

'Well, I don't know, do I?' Honestly, Dickie can be a right twit at times. '*Any* emergency ... like a fire, or someone threatening to sue the kennels – that kind of thing!'

Eventually I found my mobile and switched it on. Straightaway there was a beep. 'You've got a message.' Dickie got all excited, 'I bet our lottery numbers have come up and we're millionaires!'

'Don't talk rubbish!' I fumbled to retrieve the message. 'People like us don't win the lottery. You have to be rich already, or old and wrinkly so there's no time left to spend it.'

'Or be a jailbird, who doesn't deserve it.'

'What? Like us you mean?'

'I'm not a jailbird!'

'Yes, you are. You've been locked in a cell. If that's not being a jailbird I don't know what is.'

'Just read the message,' Dickie insisted. 'We might be rich after all.'

I read the message. 'It's from Poppy.'

'Well, what does it say?'

'Nothing!'

'Don't be daft! How can it be nothing?'

'It's nothing for you to worry about, that's all you need to know.' I rammed the mobile back into my pocket.

'What's wrong?'

'Why should anything be wrong?'

Dickie stared at me, in that all knowing, aggravating way he has, 'I don't know, but whatever she said, it seems to have got you all worked up.'

'Don't talk rubbish!' He didn't know it, but he was too close for comfort.

'Is she leaving?'

'Not that I know of.'

'Is she in trouble?'

'She didn't say.'

'I know what she said.'

'No you don't, and you're not going to!'

'Everybody knows it.'

'Knows what?'

'Poppy has the hots for you.'

I turned away, pretending to look for a café. 'There's one. Look! At the far end of the pier!'

'Tell me what she said, or I'll spread the word that we were taken in like a pair of idiots by two women.'

'You'd better not, and if you do, I'll deny it. People will believe me over you any day!'

'Okay. So I'll spread the word and you can deny it. But it won't be nice, and anyway, I've always been a better liar than you.'

That was true. Whenever I lied I couldn't help but look down to the floor, and people knew it. 'Poppy wrote … well, she said … she misses us, and that's all.'

'And?'

'She said it's been really busy.'

'What else?'

'She sounded a bit … stressed, that's all. They've been really busy.'

'Let me see.'

'You can't. I deleted it.'

'You're lying!'

Realising I was on a loser, I handed him the mobile, 'It's just like I said, she's finding it all too much. Don't read anything else into what she says. It's just talk, that's all it is. You know what Poppy's like. Sometimes she says the craziest…'

Dickie was already reading the message aloud:

Hello, Ben, how are you? I hope you're enjoying your break. It's been really busy here. We've had two litters born and I had to call out the RSPCA because there was a fox snooping about. This morning I accidentally drenched the postman and he says if I do it again, he'll refuse to come on the premises. We made him a cup of tea and he calmed down a bit, until that new dog escaped and bit him (I don't suppose he'll be sitting down for a while). We'll all be glad to see you back, especially me, because I've never had the nerve to tell you to your face, but I really like you a lot. I would love to go out with you, if you want to that is. I really hope you say yes, Lots of love, Poppy. XX

'WOW!' Giggling insanely, Dickie handed me back the mobile.

'Well, go on then,' I was waiting for the jibes, 'make something of it why don't you?'

'You know what, Ben?' Dickie looked me in the eye, 'I knew how she felt about you all along … we all did. Poppy has never had eyes for anyone but you, only you're too thick headed to see it!'

'Don't talk daft!'

'All I'm saying is … it's not every day a decent girl like Poppy pours her heart out to someone; especially to a born loser like you. If I were you I'd snap her up!'

'Are you serious?'

'She's the sweetest little thing, and she's miles better than anyone you've ever been with.'

'Leave off, Dickie! This is *Poppy* we're talking about!'

'So?'

'So, she's … well, she's *Poppy*. She's just … *Poppy*! I could never take her out on a date. She's just a kid, and anyway, I've never thought of her in that way.'

'Well then, it's time you did. And she's not just a kid. She's in her twenties already. I'll tell you something else an' all. When she's not dressed in that baggy boiler suit, mucking out the kennels or watering the yard, with her hair pulled back in a knot, she's a real cracker. A few Saturdays back, I saw her out with her mates, and she's a real looker … in fact I didn't even recognise her at first.'

I couldn't believe I was even discussing this with him. Poppy was Poppy and that was an end to it. In fact, I even felt myself thinking about what she'd written, 'Look! She's a kid with a crush. I've never been interested in her and I never will be … at least not in that way. So, if you don't mind, let's just leave it at that!'

Dickie shrugged, 'Okay, if that's the way you want it, but I think you're a fool. Here's this lovely girl throwing herself at your feet and you can't even see her for what she is.'

'Shut up, Dickie!' Desperate to change the subject, I pointed to the blackboard outside the café. 'Look! Full breakfast … just what the doctor ordered.'

It was a clean enough place, with views right out over the beach, and as we opened the door and went in, the aroma of bacon cooking smelled fantastic. 'I didn't know how hungry I was,' I said as we found ourselves a table to sit at. 'You know what, Dickie?'

'What?'

'I reckon I'll go for a full breakfast as well.'

The waiter looked like he'd had too many full breakfasts, as his belly arrived before he did. 'Morning!'

'Morning. Two full breakfasts, please.'

'Right then, lads … so it's egg, bacon, sausage, and either tomatoes or mushrooms … which is it to be?'

'Can we have both?'

'You'll have to pay the set price of £3 and another 80p on top if you do.'

We went for it. 'Oh, and two big mugs of tea, and a plate of something for the mutt, if you will, please?'

My stomach was playing a tune, 'It's busy, don't you think?'

Dickie looked round, 'There's only one empty table.'

'The food must be good then.'

And it was. Battersby got some leftover sausages, and we got what we ordered in abundance. Everything was crisp and fresh and cooked to perfection, and when we'd eaten every last crumb, the hot, strong tea washed it all down nicely.

When we went to pay the bill, we told the proprietor how much we'd enjoyed the breakfast and his grin was a mile wide. 'That's grand!' he said. 'So you'll come again, will yer?' He nodded to the many people sitting round and about. 'All regular customers,' he announced proudly, 'some of 'em have been coming here for years.'

We told him that if we were ever in the area again, we'd be certain to come back.

Then as we left, the other customers smiled and bade us good morning and I thought it was a very nice, friendly place.

Feeling much happier, we went to collect the car. On our way home, we couldn't stop talking about our trip. 'We've had an adventure if nothing else,' I said.

'We must never let on what nearly happened!' Dickie promised.

I told him, 'There's no danger of that, don't you worry.'

As we drove on to the motorway, I was thinking of Poppy's heartfelt message. I had always harboured a sneaking admiration of her and now I was seeing her like Dickie described, all dressed up, with her pretty hair loose and looking like a million dollars.

Dickie must have been reading my mind, 'You'd be a fool not to take Poppy out on a date,' he said. 'If *you* don't pick her up, somebody else will, and how would you feel about that, eh?'

I turned on the radio. There was an old recording by the Rolling Stones playing. We sang along, and Battersby howled, and for the moment I pushed Poppy out of my mind.

The very idea of taking her out seemed ridiculous, and yet. And yet?

BEDFORD
SEPTEMBER, THE FOLLOWING SATURDAY

After dithering about, I finally asked Poppy out. At first she blushed and giggled, and I felt a bit like a schoolboy with a crush.

We went to the cinema to see a re-run of Patrick Swayze in *Ghost*, and even though I wasn't into all that romance rubbish, I enjoyed it, just because Poppy was there beside me.

Hey! I'm not saying I'm in love, and I'm not saying I'm not interested in seeing her again, because I am, but after the horror of Laura and Nancy, I'd rather take it slowly, slowly.

All I will say is that when I walked her up the steps to her parents' house, she turned to say goodnight and I knew Dickie was right. She was really pretty, and so sweet, I didn't want to leave her.

'Goodnight, Ben,' she whispered, 'I've had a wonderful time.'

'So have I.' I felt ten feet tall. 'D'you think we could do it again soon?'

Her answer was to kiss me long and tenderly on the mouth.

It wasn't the kind of fiery kiss that set your heart alight, nor was it too suggestive. It was just a beautiful kiss, one that said I love you, but let's take it slowly.

And that's all right with me, because you know what? I can see myself falling hook, line and sinker for this very special girl. After all the mistakes I've made, I really feel as though I've found the right girl, at long last.

I went down the street with a spring in my step and a song in my heart. I just knew that this was the start of something big.

'Good on you, Dickie,' I murmured, 'I'm so glad I took your advice!' I even started singing.

Suddenly, out of nowhere this shower of rotten apples rained down on me, bursting all over my head and splashing my best trousers. All this gunk and stinking stuff dripped down my face and into my eyes, until I could hardly see; it was like something out of a horror movie.

Suddenly a familiar voice boomed out, 'BASTARD! I SAW YOU AND 'ER KISSING LIKE TWO LOVESICK PIGEONS. I WON'T HAVE IT! D'YOU HEAR! YOU'RE MINE, BEN BUSKIN, AND IF I CAN'T HAVE YOU, NO ONE ELSE WILL! I know I divorced you, but I'm not done yet!!'

'LAURA! You mad cow, what the hell d'you think you're doing?' Spluttering and coughing, I tried to stand up, but the apples kept coming and I couldn't keep my balance.

The onslaught stopped as suddenly as it had started.

For a while I stayed there, scraping the gunk off; my head spinning with her threats. 'You're off your trolley!' I shouted after her. But I was determined. She can do whatever she likes, but I was free of her. She had no hold over me whatsoever. If I want to go out with Poppy, I will, and if I decide to ask her to marry me, I will. In fact, the idea seemed more attractive by the minute.

I got into the car, switched on the engine and shifted into gear. 'Mad as a hatter!' I muttered. 'She wants locking up!'

I was furious, 'It'd do her good to be put in a cell like me and Dickie.'

That got me thinking about the past few days, and a little smile spread, and then I was laughing out loud. 'I'm a disaster area!'

But you know what?

I'm just glad to be alive, and if my crazy control freak of an ex thinks she can stop me from seeing Poppy, she's got another thing coming, because from now on, nobody, but nobody is going to tell me what to do!

When I got home, I discovered that she'd let all my tyres down. The thing is, I thought that funny, flapping sound

239

was my stomach rumbling. I guess I was lost in Poppy's kiss!

WHAT AM I LIKE!

Read on for an exclusive extract of Josephine's
New novel Blood Brothers, out now in hardback
and coming in paperback in
October 2010

BLOOD BROTHERS

CHAPTER ONE

GENTLY CRADLING THE injured bird, he stood on the high ground, his quiet gaze drawn to the field below.

Up there, in the windswept heights, he cut a fine figure of a man. He was not broad of shoulder, nor thick with muscle, but there was something about him, a certain strength and solitude, and the tall, proud manner in which he stood.

He was a man of integrity. He knew when to speak his mind and when to keep his silence. He also knew when to walk away.

A year ago, he had done exactly that, yet against his better instincts, he had answered his brother's letter and made his way back. Even now he felt uneasy in this familiar place, with his family less than a mile away, and Alice just a few steps from where he now stood.

It seemed he had been away forever. A year ago he left this haven to travel far and wide to search for a quietness of heart that might allow him to build a new life and move on. Yet all he ever found was loneliness.

Out here, in the wide open skies and with only the wild creatures for company, he was at home.

When he was away, this was what he missed. This . . . and a woman who was not his, and never could be.

Now that he was so close to home, he still wasn't sure he had done the right thing. 'It might have been better if I'd stayed away . . .'

Deep down he had always known it would not be easy, seeing her again. Yet now, here he was and she was just a heartbeat away. Thankfully, she had not yet seen him.

He whispered her name, '*Alice.*' Her name was oddly comforting on his lips, '*Alice.*'

After a while he moved into the spinney where he kept watch, secure in the knowledge that she could not see him.

Discreetly, he continued to watch her through the branches of the ancient trees. He shared her joy as she raced across the field, her green skirt billowing in the breeze, her long chestnut-coloured hair playing over her shoulders. Behind her the lambs followed like children, calling and skipping as she led them, like a pied piper, down to the water's edge.

His thoughtful brown eyes followed her every step. She was the reason he had turned his back on friends and family, and yet it was not her fault, for she had done nothing wrong.

While he was away he had come to realise that whatever he did, wherever he went, she would be there; like the blood that coursed through his veins.

He saw her now; small, strappy shoes clutched in one hand, her skirt held high as she paddled barefoot through the cool-running stream. He blinked at the sun in the skies; he felt the warmth on his face, and for one magic moment the world stood still.

Oblivious to his presence, she rested herself on a boulder, her two arms stretched out and her head back, as she raised her face to the heavens. She made no move to collect the hem of her skirt as it dipped into the water. Instead she stretched out her bare legs to let the cool, frothing water trickle over her skin.

When a stray lamb drew close enough to nuzzle her neck, she tenderly reached out to caress its tiny face.

In this green and glorious landscape, wrapped in silence and surrounded by nature's beauty, she seemed at one with all creation.

For a fleeting moment, when she seemed to lift her gaze his way, he feared she had seen him, yet he made no move. In truth, he could not tear himself away. He had to see her, to fill his senses with her simple beauty. Little more than a year ago she had unknowingly opened his heart and crept inside, and now she was etched there for all time.

It pained him to realise that soon he must turn away and be gone from here. This time, never to return.

For now though, the moment, and the woman, were his. Up here, above the hubbub and maelstrom of ordinary life, time did not exist. It was just the two of them, and that was how it should be. She belonged only to him.

Content, he closed his eyes and let the feelings flow through him. He wished the world might stand still for this one, precious moment. Or maybe even forever.

The guilt was never far away: for his was a love both forbidden and wicked.

He spent every waking moment wanting her. She was the last thought on his mind when he went to sleep, and the first thought on his mind when he woke.

She had caused him such turmoil.

That was what she did to him.

Fearful, the injured bird fluttered in his arms, desperate to escape. 'Ssh!' He looked down into those piercing dark eyes that twinkled up at him. 'She's much like you,' he whispered. 'Wild as the wind; part of the earth itself.'

Acutely aware of the need to tend the bird's injury, he was loath to tear himself away. So he lingered awhile, watching as she waded ankle-deep through the water and on to the far bank. Behind her, the lambs continued to graze on the moist grass.

'She's away to the farmhouse!' Drawing the small creature nearer to his chest, he carefully folded its damaged wing into the palm of his hand. 'We'd best make our way there too.' He stroked its feathers with the tip of his thumb, 'Let's hope we can get you flying again.'

Carrying the bird gently he took the shortest route: down the hill and across the stream, carefully negotiating the stones and boulders as he went.

Soon he caught sight of Alice, running through the long grass, her voice lifted in song. It made him smile.

He continued on, to the farmhouse; the place where he grew up.

The place where he first met Alice.

The anger was like a fist inside him, '. . . yearning after a woman who's already promised to your brother is a dangerous thing,' he murmured.

Though what he felt for Alice was more than a yearning. It was a raging fire that, try as he might, he could not put out.

With the farmhouse in sight, he grew anxious; remembering why he was here. He was sobered by the knowledge that in just a few short days he would stand at the altar, where Alice and his brother would be pronounced man and wife.

It was a prospect he would rather not dwell on.

~

'I wonder if he's on his way?'

Bustling about in the cosy farmhouse kitchen, Nancy Arnold walked over to the window. A small, round woman of fifty years and more, she had the cheekiest, chubbiest face, pretty dark eyes wrinkled with laughter-lines, and a long thick plait of dark brown hair, lightly peppered with grey.

She was a woman of high standards; a woman who stood no nonsense and took no prisoners. Yet she was the kindest, most understanding woman on earth. When the neighbours suffered ill-health or encountered trouble she was the first to lend a helping hand.

And when attending a merry occasion, she could out-sing and outdance any man or woman; her manner and laughter was so infectious her husband Tom claimed she was shaking the ground with her terrible screeching! Her laughter filled his heart, and he loved her more with every passing year.

'Stop wittering, woman!' he grumbled at her now. 'Sit yer busy backside down an' give us a bit o' quiet!' Peering over his newspaper, he firmly chided. 'Your son will be 'ere when he gets 'ere, and all yer fussing and fretting won't get him here any the sooner!' Having lived in the countryside all his life, Tom had learned to take things as they came.

'Aw, Tom, I'm that worried.'

She turned to look at him. 'We should have had word by now. The wedding's on Saturday. It's Monday already; less than a week to go, and we've heard not a whisper from him. What if he can't get 'ere? What if he's had an accident on the way . . . oh dearie me!'

'Hey!' Crumpling the newspaper to his knee, Tom wagged a finger at her. 'We'll have none o' that kind of talk! Why don't yer make us a nice cup of tea, eh? Happen it'll calm yer nerves.'

'The only thing that'll calm my nerves is the sight of our Joe coming through that door.'

'Mebbe, but watching out for him every two minutes won't bring him 'ere any the quicker.' With his large frame, thick, beard and piercing blue eyes, Tom Arnold was a man of fierce appearance, though like his wife, he had a soft heart.

In no time at all the kettle was whistling on the hob, and Nancy had brewed a pot of tea. She got out the tray, along with two mugs, into which she spooned a generous helping of sugar, then a drop of milk for Tom, and a good measure for herself. After that she took a small plate from the cupboard and sliding four ginger-snaps on to it, she rearranged the whole lot on the tray, before waddling over to the table. 'There y'are then!' She plonked the tray unceremoniously before him. 'So, is there anything else you want?'

'Nope, except for you to sit still. Yer making my nerves bad. First yer at the window, then yer at the door, then yer upstairs at the window again. Then yer 'ere and now yer there, and soon yer off somewheres else. In and out, up and down, making me that dizzy I can't settle to read my blessed paper. Why can't you sit down, drink your tea and be patient?'

'Don't be like that.' Already on her way to the window again, she looked at him in a way that usually melted his heart. But not this time. This time he was desperate to pick out his horses for today's race. 'I know I'm a fidget, but I can't help it,' she complained. 'I'm on edge d'you see?'

She paused, feeling as though she had the weight of the world on her mind. 'Tom?'

He groaned. 'What now?'

'I really am worried.'

'Well you shouldn't be!' Frustrated, he rolled his eyes to heaven. 'Like I said, our Joe will turn up. In any case, as long as he gets here before Saturday morning, it'll be fine. Stop panicking, woman!'

'It's not just about Joe being late,' she replied quietly. 'There's something else . . .'

'Something else?' Now, he was interested. 'Come on then. Let's have it!'

Nancy had not planned to say anything, but it was on her mind and she needed reassurance. 'Has it never puzzled you why our Joe took off like he did,' she asked. 'I mean . . . one minute he was 'ere, and then he were gone, just like that, without any explanation.'

'I did wonder at the time, but I can't say I've lost any sleep over it. Besides, young men are notoriously unpredictable, so don't worry about it. Anyway, I'm sure he had his reasons.'

That was not good enough for Nancy. 'The way I see it, if he could go off on a whim like that at the drop of a hat, without any explanation, who's to say he'll not have another whim and decide to stay away?'

'Because his brother tracked him down a month back and asked him to be his best man, that's why! Like I say, Joe won't let his brother down, and well you know it.'

'He didn't write back straightaway though, did he? It was a whole month before Frank got a reply.'

'Yes, but that's only because like all other young men, Joe is not a letter writer.'

'What if he doesn't *want* to be best man at his brother's wedding?'

'Don't be daft, woman!' Tom put his newspaper aside. 'What the devil's got into you, Nancy?'

'I just wondered, that's all.'

'About what?'

Nancy shrugged her shoulders. 'I'm not really sure. It's just that when Joe left I got the feeling he was upset about something. You remember a couple of nights before he left, Joe was introduced to Alice? Oh, he smiled and gave her a kiss and everything seemed fine. Only, after that, he was too quiet for my liking.'

She recalled it only too well. 'He hardly said two words over dinner, then he went to bed early.'

'That's because he'd been working out in the field all day, doing the work of three men. Me and the farmhand were away at the market with the calves, and as you recall, Frank had hurt his back. On top of that, it was the hottest day of summer. Joe was drenched with sweat and completely done-in when he finally got home. Frank was all excited because he'd brought Alice home and straightaway she was thrust under Joe's nose. He was even made to welcome her with a kiss, and him being so shy an' all!' Tom gave a hearty chuckle, 'I can't say I'm surprised he had little to say for himself!'

'But it wasn't like Joe to be so quiet,' Nancy insisted. 'The following morning I got up early, determined to find out what was troubling him. When I came down, he was already packed and gone, leaving only a scrap of a letter by the kettle to say he was off to see the world.'

'He wrote and put your mind at rest though, didn't he?' She shook her head. 'He's always put duty first before,' Tom replied reassuringly.

'From what I recall about his letter, Joe seemed happy enough,' Tom reminded her. 'He was making good money working the fairground, and he'd palled up with another lad. So, when the boss offered them the chance to go to Europe with the fair, they jumped at it!' He chuckled. 'I don't mind telling yer . . . if I'd been offered the same chance when I were Joe's age, I'd have been gone like a shot!'

'So, you think the only reason he left was because he wanted to see the world?' Nancy asked.

'That's *exactly* what I think, yes.' Tom was not a natural liar, but he had to put Nancy's mind to rest.

The last thing he wanted to do was alarm her with his own suspicions about why Joe left.

In fact his thoughts on the matter were so unsettling, he had never once shared them with Nancy.

Nancy was like a dog with a bone. 'Are you sure he didn't say anything to you?' she persisted. 'About why he was rushing away, or where he was headed?'

'He said nothing to me, but like I'm telling you, it's likely he wanted to see what the big wide world had to offer before he settled down.'

Tom thought of his own life and how his world had only ever been this farm, rented from the landowner by his grandfather and father before him. 'I remember when *I* were twenty-five,' he remarked thoughtfully. 'I were still working the land morning 'til night, seven days a week.'

'Ah, yes, but that was then and this is now,' Nancy reminded him. 'Times change, don't forget that.'

'I'm not likely to, because here I am, an old man plagued with aching bones and a nagging wife. I've two

254

grown sons: one of 'em's fled the nest, and the other's straining at the leash to get wed. I've a heap o' responsibility weighing me down, an' after all these years hard work, I haven't even managed to buy a house to call our own!'

Nancy was taken aback by his outburst. 'In all the years we've been married, I've never once heard you talk like that.' It worried her. 'Are you saying you regret your life?'

'Absolutely not!' Giving her a reassuring wink, Tom reached out and kissed her on the mouth, before revealing sincerely, 'I don't regret a single minute of it, and as for you and my boys, you *are* my life. That's what it's all been about and still is. And there isn't a day passes that I don't give thanks.'

Feeling emotional, Nancy told him passionately, 'You're such a good man, Tom.' She gave him a look that only a woman in love could give. 'Since you first asked me to dance at the village hall, I felt proud to be with you. I always will.'

'Thank you, sweetheart.' He smiled into those pretty brown eyes. 'I'm proud of you an' all, and I'm proud of our two sons. Different though they may be, they're both good, fine fellows.'

'Tom?' There was something else playing on her mind.

'What now, sweetheart?' He so wanted to get back to his horses.

'Don't take this the wrong way, but I was wondering, what d'you think to Alice? Do you really think her and

Frank will be happy together?'

'Mmm . . .' He chose his words carefully. 'If I'm honest, I reckon she might be a bit young. She's not yet twenty, and Frank is nearly seven years older. That said, she thinks the world of our Frank, and he adores her. So what do a few years matter, eh?'

'So, you really think she's the right one for our son?'

Remembering what he had witnessed that night a year ago, Tom chose his words carefully. 'Well now, I don't have a crystal ball, but I would say Alice has the true makings of a farmer's wife.'

He paused, remembering how calm and helpful Alice had been when they had had a bad incident with a month-old foal. 'D'you recall how that young postman ran to tell us how Alice was in trouble and needed help? Youngsters from the town had smashed part of the fence down at the far field, and one of the foals had got caught up in it?'

Nancy recalled it vividly. 'Its mother was running crazy, and wouldn't let anyone near.'

He reminded her, 'I reckon that mad mare would have killed anyone who went near her young 'un. The vet couldn't get anywhere near until Alice calmed the mare long enough for him to tend the foal.'

Nancy remembered it well. 'She's certainly got a way with animals. She's not afraid of hard work neither. All in all, I think you're right. Young Alice will fit in with the family very nicely.'

She added reluctantly, 'I'm not sure Joe approves of her though.'

Tom was surprised. 'What put that idea into yer head?'

'I might be wrong,' she replied thoughtfully, 'only I got the feeling that he would rather she wasn't here, that's all.'

Tom was quick to dispel her fears. 'Honestly, Nancy. Fancy thinking our Joe would take a dislike to a girl who wouldn't harm a fly! I expect he had his head so full of adventure, he didn't even notice her!'

Nancy seemed relieved. 'Yes, that must have been it. Forget what I said.'

Tom watched her as she ambled across the room. Leaning her elbows on the window sill, she gave a soft laugh. 'Hey! Wouldn't it be something if he turned up with a girl on his arm?'

'I shouldn't think our Joe will bring a woman home just yet,' he told Nancy now. He then muttered under his breath, 'Why would he do that, when the girl he fancies is right here?'

Tom had long suspected that was why Joe had gone away: because he had fallen for his brother's woman, and he couldn't deal with it. Neither could Tom, for it was a terrible, shameful thing.

All the same, Tom understood how sometimes love grabs you when you least expect it, and no one could control who they fall in love with.

He didn't blame Joe. He didn't blame anyone; though he had secretly admired his son for doing the right thing in putting a distance between himself and Alice.

He felt a sense of unease. 'I hope to God our Joe's over her. If not, it could really put the cat among the pigeons!' he whispered to himself.

'What was that you said?' Nancy swung round.

'What?' Pretending he was deep in his newspaper, Tom looked up, '*I* didn't say anything!'

'I thought you said something about a cat among the pigeons?'

'Naw. Yer must be getting old. Hearing voices in yer head now is it?'

Sighing, Nancy ambled back to her chair. 'I'm all wound up,' she said, 'I'll be all right when Joe gets here.'

As Nancy sipped her tea, Tom took a moment to look at her. As a girl she was much like Alice: the same long brown hair and inquisitive mind. She hadn't changed that much, he thought. Yes, she was plumper, and the dark hair was sprinkled with grey, but when she smiled, the years flew away, and it was the girl he saw.

Laying his hand on hers, he kissed her tenderly on the cheek, and never said a word. He didn't have to, because she knew already.

'You're an old softie, that's what you are.' She smiled up at him, 'And you're right about our sons. They *are* different; I've always thought Joe took after you, and Frank is more in the nature of your father. He'll see a lamb all caught up and rescue it, but it's not the lamb he's rescuing, it's the money it'll fetch at market.'

'Well o'course! He's a farmer, and that's how *any* farmer would think, even though he's not altogether conscious of it.'

'I know that, but what I'm saying is, Joe would rescue the same lamb yes, but only because it pains him to see it caught up. The money it might bring at market wouldn't even enter his head.'

Tom nodded. 'Aye well, there yer have it. You see, our Frank has the same attitude as my own father, and there is nothing wrong with that! It shows he's a hard-headed businessman. He sees everything in black and white, while Joe takes time to see the shades and the colours.'

'Oh, and you don't?' She smiled knowingly.

'Give over, woman. I've no time for all that!'

Embarrassed, he grabbed his newspaper and hid behind it. 'I need some new specs,' he grumbled. 'The print on the pages gets smaller by the minute!'

Gently, Nancy drew the newspaper away. 'You don't fool me, Tom Arnold.' She knew him like she knew herself.

Feigning anger, he wagged a finger. 'Look! It's hard enough to keep a family going if the crops are ruined or you lose an animal. Survival! That's the thing, and don't you be mekking any more of it!'

Snatching his newspaper he again buried his head in it. 'Go on! Away to the window and watch for Joe!'

As she prepared to move away, he caught her by the arm. 'I hope you know how much I love you, and how lucky I am to have yer,' he declared stoutly.

'Right, well just you remember that when you're yelling at me.'

Her comment made him smile. 'When have I ever

yelled at you?'

'Hmm. Have you got all day?'

Chuckling, he folded the newspaper and laid it on the arm of the chair,

A few minutes later, after returning from her disappointing vigil at the window, she came to sit beside him. 'It'll be so good to have our Joe home.'

Having settled herself into the chair, she sipped her lukewarm tea, while at the same time observing the state of the painted walls. 'How long is it since these walls were painted?' she asked.

'Long time.' Tom peeked over his newspaper. 'Six or seven years . . . maybe more.'

Tom had to agree the place was looking the worse for wear, but he would never admit it.

'Folks might think it all a bit jaded, that's all I'm saying,' Nancy pointed out.

'What folks think is no concern of ours.' Tom declared. 'You need to remember, this place doesn't belong to us. I'm sure that tight-fisted landlord won't be shelling out money if he can help it, and *we* certainly can't afford to redecorate. Not with the wedding coming up an' all.'

'Ah, well, not to worry, eh?' Nancy was a sensible woman, and right now she had more important things on her mind. 'Let's just hope nobody comes back here after the celebration.' She gave him a cheeky wink. 'If they do, they'll have to accept us as we are. As long as the wedding goes without a hitch, it doesn't really matter.'

'There won't be any hitches,' he promised cheerfully. 'Not with you in charge, and half the village wanting to help.'

Nancy gave no reply to that, although she knew from experience that things could go so easily wrong. In her usual forthright manner, she had learned to take nothing for granted.

She proudly informed him, 'Everything has been well organised. Flowers are arranged and paid for. The band is booked, and the suits for you and the boys are hanging in the closet; though Joe's might need a tweak here and there, depending on whether he's changed his shape since we last saw him.'

Tom was duly impressed. 'Sounds to me like you've thought of everything.'

'I hope so. I've gone over the menu for the meal, and now there's just the wedding-cake. Seeing as I'm baking it, the cost is half what it would have been if I'd ordered one.'

She gave a little scowl. 'It's as well I'm doing the cake, because even Alice had to admit that her mother is a terrible cook. Apparently, she can't even produce a proper Yorkshire pud!'

Tom chuckled. 'There y'are y'see. It's just as well you're available then, isn't it?'

In fact, Nancy felt well pleased with herself. 'Mind you, Alice's mother played her part in helping Alice choose the flowers. Though she wasn't able to make Alice change her mind about having wild flowers in amongst the tulips and such. To be honest I reckon a mixture of colourful wild flowers will look absolutely gorgeous!'

There was one other thing. 'In the end though Alice didn't get much of a say in the wedding dress, she did manage to lose the idea of frills and bows like her mother wanted. Instead the dress will be sewn with daisies and forget-me-nots . . . all made out of silk and satin.'

Tom smiled in agreement. 'Alice is a simple country girl at heart,' he said softly. 'She won't have her head turned by expense and fancy, and I'm proud of that! If you ask me, she'll walk down the aisle looking like a million dollars!'

Nancy's thoughts had already turned again to her youngest son. 'Everything is ready now.' She glanced anxiously towards the window. 'All we need is for Joe to show his face.'

Having had enough of the cold tea, she was quickly away, watching at the window again. 'He'll not show while you're watching,' Tom groaned. 'Anyway, I thought you had umpteen jobs to get done?'

'They can wait.' She ran her finger over the smeared window. 'Tom Arnold!' Swinging round she confronted him. 'You promised faithfully you would clean the windows, and they've not even been touched!'

'Sorry, love. I'll do it later.' Shame-faced, he buried his head in his newspaper. 'Just give me a few minutes, and I'll get on with it . . . soon as I've chosen the winning horses.'

Minutes passed, and still there was no sign of Joe.

'You're right again,' she muttered. 'A watched kettle never boils.'

Just then she caught sight of Alice. 'Oh, look!' Pointing as though Tom could see from across the room, she told him, 'There's Alice. For a minute I thought it might be our Joe coming out of the barn.'

'Give over, woman! If he *is* on his way back, he'd hardly make the barn his first stop, now would he?'

Returning to his newspaper, he blocked his ears to Nancy's running commentary. 'No doubt she's off to collect the early apples. They're keepers d'you see? If you leave them too late the insects burrow in, and they're not worth tuppence. But pick them before they ripen and they'll come up a treat after a few weeks in the barn.'

'Don't teach your grandmother to suck eggs.' Tom had to put her right. 'I were collecting keeper-apples when you were still in nappies.'

'Oh, dear me I forgot!' She gave him a derisory glance. 'There's nothing *you* can teach me about farming is there, eh?'

'Nope.'

'So, what about the potatoes last season? I suggested we get the potato crop in before the rains came, and you argued that the weather would be absolutely fine for at least another week. Two days later the skies burst open and it poured for days. So thanks to you we lost half the crop.'

He suffered her teasing for the next few minutes, while intermittently nodding and grunting, as though he was paying attention. If she paused he'd look up and say, 'Really . . . well fancy that!'

'I feel awful now.' Nancy returned to the wedding. 'I promised Alice I'd give her a hand with bringing the apples in, but there's been so much on my mind I completely forgot.'

'She won't mind.'

In spite of his concerns with regard to Joe, he truly believed that in Alice, Frank had found himself the makings of a fine wife.

~

Alice had just placed the last of the keepers into the basket when she saw Joe going into the barn. She called out after him. Collecting the basket, she ran out of the orchard and along the shingle path to the big barn.

At the doorway she peered inside, and there was Joe, tenderly stroking the injured bird. 'We'll get you right,' he told it softly. 'You'll soon be able to spread your wings and soar through the skies where you belong.'

Suddenly aware of someone watching him, he turned quickly. 'Hello, Joe,' she said softly. Putting the basket to the ground, Alice came forward, her face bright with a smile. 'I wasn't sure it was you at first. I only ever saw you the once, and then you were gone. That was a year ago now, wasn't it?' She remembered their first meeting, how quiet and shy he seemed, and how each time she glanced up, he was looking at her. There was something about Frank's younger brother that made her nervous. For a long time after he left, she found herself missing him.

For a moment, Joe didn't say anything. Instead he thought of that fateful day when Frank brought her home, and how he couldn't take his eyes off her. And yes, it may have been a year ago, but to him it was like only yesterday.

So many times of late he had hoped that when he saw her again things might be different, but they weren't. The feelings he had then were still there, haunting him. The very sight of her made his heart beat faster, and his throat was so dry he could hardly breathe.

'Alice!' He felt foolish, not really knowing what to say. 'I'm sorry. I didn't see you there.'

Closing the distance between them, she smiled up at him. 'That's because you were so intent on comforting the bird.'

Reaching out, she stroked the bird along its velvet, feathery neck. 'He's a *falcon*, isn't he?'

'That's right,' Joe confirmed. 'I don't think he's long out of the nest. Maybe he hasn't yet learned the art of diving for his prey.'

'What's wrong with him?' Whenever a creature was hurt, Alice felt it deeply. Sometimes, when she was worried or feeling lonely, the creatures gave her a great sense of peace and timelessness.

Even as a child, she had always felt far safer with animals than with any human – including her parents.

She thought of her mother, always arguing and fighting, thinking only of herself. She was a cold person, cold and selfish. Yet she could not hate her, nor could she love her. That was her deepest regret.

'Is he badly hurt?' She turned her attention to the falcon.

'His wing is damaged, but I think he'll be okay,' Joe assured her.

Alice glanced along the run of stables where the two work-horses had their heads over the doors and were looking out. 'You could put him in the empty stable.'

Joe had already seen that possibility. 'I'll need to protect him from the cats and foxes.' He looked about him. 'There should be an old cage in here. It used to belong to my pet rabbit when I was a boy.'

'I know it!' Excited, she ran the full length of the barn and there, behind some old corn barrels, she located it: a small, wooden box with a door at the side. 'Here it is!' Pulling it out, she stood it on the barrel. 'It doesn't look broken or anything.' She continued to examine it as Joe made his way down.

'It's perfect!' Placing the fluttering bird in Alice's safe hands, Joe quickly filled the cage with a bed of hay, then he rummaged about until he found a suitable piece of cane, which he used for a splint. Skilfully shaving off the sharp edges, he then snapped off a length of bale twine and while Alice held the bird close, he secured the splint along the falcon's damaged wing. 'That should hold.'

Collecting the bird from Alice, he placed it in the cage and secured the door. He then searched for something to fill with water. 'This'll do!' After unscrewing the deep lid from the top of an old storage jar, he went to the side of the barn where he washed it out under the tap, then he filled the container with water and placed it inside the cage near to the falcon.

'Oh look!' Alice was thrilled when the injured bird shuffled slowly along and, stretching out to reach the water, took a drink.

'That's good!' Joe was relieved. 'He'll be fine now. I'm just wondering . . . maybe he'd be safer inside the house until his wing is mended?'

'No!' Alice rejected the idea. 'I know he might be safer,' she agreed, 'but he would be so unhappy. He should never be put inside. Make him safe out here, where he won't be too afraid. Please, Joe?'

When Joe looked down into those strong, blue eyes, he was deeply moved. 'You're absolutely right,' he told her. 'I wasn't thinking.'

Quickly, he created a large harness out of a length of steel strapping. That done, he then secured it round the cage, and strung the cage from the rafters. 'That way, it'll be even more difficult for the foxes and cats to get at him.'

Together they went out of the barn and into the bright sunlight. There was something unique between them: a friendship born from shared experience.

Or something else, which was destined to have far-reaching and tragic consequences.

Inside the farmhouse, Tom was at the end of his tether. 'Will you come away from that damned window. You're making me nervous, to-ing and fro-ing, grumbling and muttering!'

He gave her an ultimatum. 'Either you find something else to do, other than stand at the window fretting, or I'm off out down the pub to find a bit o' peace . . .'

Nancy was past listening, because now she was hopping up and down on the spot, shouting at the top of her voice. 'He's here!' With a screech of delight, she was out the door, leaving Tom with a parting rebuke, 'I said he'd be here and I was right!'

Ambling to the door he watched as she ran headlong into Joe's open arms. 'That's put a smile on her face.' He observed Joe's tall, capable figure, and that easy manner he had, and he felt proud. 'Your mother's missed you, son,' he whispered. 'We all have.'

He remained at the door for a moment, a smile on his face as he watched Joe swing his mother round in a hug. 'It's damned good to see you, Joe,' he nodded his head. 'When all's said and done, it's only right that you should be here to stand beside your brother.'

He began his way down the path, his gaze intent on Joe and Alice as they talked and laughed together.

Seeing them so close and natural had a deep, unsettling effect on him. Instinctively, he glanced towards the fields, looking for his eldest son; relieved to see that Frank was nowhere in sight, because if he had been, he would not have failed to see the magnetism between these two.

As he got nearer to the little group, Tom continued to chatter to himself, his voice a mingling of sadness and anger. 'I'm no fool, Joe. Don't think I didn't see how you were, the first time you saw Alice. I'm sure you didn't mean it to happen. I know you would never do anything to hurt your brother. That's why you put a distance between yourself and Alice, but I can see now, you still have feelings for her.'

His voice hardened. 'Remember, son . . . Alice and Frank are to be wed on Saturday, and you'll be there to hand over the ring. In the eyes of the Lord and all that's legal, they'll be man and wife, and like it or not, you'll be expected to give them your blessing.'

There was nothing more he wanted than to have all his family together. But thankfully, that was not about to happen. Besides, with two men, living under the same roof and wanting the same woman? His old heart sank. That would be a recipe for trouble, and no mistake!

'Tom!' Alice came running up the path to meet him. 'Look! Joe's here!' Taking him by the hand, they approached Nancy and Joe, Alice all the while chattering excitedly. 'I knew he wouldn't let us down.'

Thrilled that at long last he was here to be Frank's best man at their wedding, Alice reached up to kiss him on the cheek. 'I forgot to thank you, Joe.'

'Joe found an injured falcon,' she informed them. 'He's made it safe in his old rabbit hutch.'

Joe was quick to hug his dad. 'It's really good to see you and Mum,' he said fondly. 'You're both looking well.'

'So are you, son, and I'll want to know all about your travels later on.' For now, he was interested in Joe's find. 'What's all this about an injured falcon?'

'Looks like a young one,' Joe explained. 'We've put a splint on its wing and bedded it down with a dish of water.' He glanced towards the barn, 'Given a few days I reckon it'll be just fine.'

Tom grinned. 'You haven't changed, son,' he said fondly. 'You always did have a soft spot for anything injured.'

Glancing at his parents, Joe thought they hadn't aged a day since he last saw them. 'Look, Dad . . . Mum, I'm sorry I couldn't make it earlier . . .' he apologised. 'Only . . . I had things to do . . .'

'We understand, Joe love, and it's all right. All that matters is that you're home for the wedding,' Nancy said warmly.

'I'm glad to be here,' Joe answered, though having seen Alice again, he suddenly wasn't so sure.

Just a short while ago, he had started to feel more confident about being here. Until Alice had kissed him. With the warmth of her lips still burning his face, he realised more than ever how coming back here was a bad mistake.

But it was too late now. For all sorts of reasons.

Not a man for hugging, Tom gave his son a fond pat on the back. 'Come on in, son. You can tell us what you've been up to.'

As the two of them went ahead, Nancy and Alice followed just a few steps behind.

Once inside the farmhouse, there was a real air of excitement. 'Shall I go and get Frank?' Alice asked eagerly. 'He's setting out the fencing posts in the top field.'

Tom thought that was a good idea. 'Although, that fence needs finishing, but I expect you'd best run off and fetch him. No doubt he'll be keen to see his brother. Matter o' fact, he might want to take him into Bedford.' He noticed how Joe had only a canvas bag, which was strung over his shoulder and appeared to be half empty. 'Happen Joe might need to buy a new shirt or two?'

Nancy was having none of it, 'Frank is not taking him anywhere! At least not yet. Joe's only just arrived. He must be worn out and hungry. Let him rest while I get us all something to eat.'

Turning to Alice, she informed her, 'Oh, and by the way, Frank isn't in the top field. I saw him earlier on. By the manner of his route, I imagine he was away to plough the rough area down by the brook.'

Alice thanked her. 'I won't be long,' she promised. 'I'll tell him he's to come home, and that we're all taking time out for something to eat . . . is that all right?'

Nancy smiled. 'That's it. Oh, and don't you forget what I said . . . no paddling in the brook. You might frighten the ducks.'

At that Alice laughed. 'They don't mind me,' she said.

While Joe was watching the two women, Tom noticed how Joe's gaze was instinctively drawn to Alice. Just before, when Alice thanked Joe with that innocent little kiss on the cheek, Tom sensed it had unsettled him.

It was nothing glaringly obvious, and it didn't seem to have attracted anyone's notice as such. Even Alice herself had not realised the effects of that grateful little kiss.

Tom had felt it though; just like before when Joe was first introduced to Alice. There was a kind of under-current; a strong, palpable presence that wrapped the two of them together and excluded everyone else from the room.

It was a dangerous thing, and one that deeply worried him.

It was painfully obvious to Tom that his youngest son still harboured strong feelings for his brother's woman. If anything, his absence had only fuelled the need in him.

He was grateful that for the moment at least, both Alice and Nancy had failed to sense anything untoward.

The truth was, he didn't really know how to deal with it, other than sending his son away; right now, with the wedding so near and everyone excitedly looking forward to it, that was no easy option. Besides, he didn't have the heart to do such a thing.

All he could do was keep a close eye on things, because one thing was certain. Here was a worrying situation, which could easily escalate out of hand.

Emotions were powerful things. They could cripple a man.

And sometimes, however hard that man might try, it was hard to keep control.